The Spy Who Did Not Know

Vern Kaska III

Vkwork publishing— Larkspur, CO
ISBN: 979-8-218-07373-2
Library of Congress Control Number: 2022917541
Title: *The Spy Who Did Not Know*
Author: Vern Kaska III
Digital distribution | 2022
Paperback | 2022

Dedication

This book is dedicated to all the long flights and nights in a hotel room traveling for work. This allowed me the free time I needed to write my first book.

Chapter One
The Setup

As he lay there running his finger slowly down her breast, he started to realize that this was different than all the other times before. He wasn't already thinking about the next mission and was content to lay with her all night. Although she was younger, she was not immature and needy like most girls. Seducing her was easy. This would usually be an annoyance for him as he loves a good challenge.

Earlier that day in the market he was standing there with two bottles in his hand looking rather confused, so much so he almost looked like he was about to cry. She couldn't help herself. Normally she would not engage with a tourist, but he looked so out of sorts she felt she must help.

"Are you okay, sir?"

"Um, well I think so. Would you be able to recommend a good bottle of wine?"

"What are you cooking?" the woman smiled.

"I'm not quite sure what will be for dinner. I just want to show up with a nice bottle of wine. I believe that is the proper thing to do when invited to dinner in France. I'm not much of a wine drinker myself as you can probably tell."

"Well, if you're not the cook then I would recommend putting the cooking wine back on the shelf, leaving the market and going to a place that serves drinking wine not cooking wine."

He closed his eyes, and with a look of embarrassment said, "Man, I cannot get anything right in this city."

She laughed as he put the bottles back. "How is it you are in France and know nothing about wine?"

"How about you take me to a place and help me pick out a bottle of wine? Then I will repay you with lunch and the most uninteresting story you have ever heard. Now, how can you resist that?" he asked, with a playful smile.

"I am meeting my father for dinner tonight," she said. She could see the disappointment on his face, but she had learned at an early age not to get involved with the tourist as they are always here today and gone tomorrow and usually only looking for one thing in the city of love.

"Okay, well thank you for stopping me from making this colossal mistake. Can you please point me in the right direction?" he asked.

"You need to go to Au Nouveau Nez."

"AA Nouvato des?" he said.

She laughed, "You are hopeless."

She could not believe she was going to break her rule, although he did not seem to be making a move on her. Maybe he was just a nice man looking for some help.

"Okay," she laughed, raising her hands in mock surrender. "I'll take you and help you pick out a bottle, but after that, you are on your own.

He let out a big sigh of relief and said, "Thank you."

She took the sigh of relief that he was thankful for the help, but he was thinking, that was way too easy, and this is going to be another mind-numbing day.

"Please lead the way," he said.

"I think a cab will be best," she said, as she started to

lead them out of the store.

"I thought this place was famous for wine is it not everywhere?" he asked with a puzzled look on his face.

"Well, I am of the belief if you are going to do something you do it right. Plus, I have a most uninteresting story to hear on the way," she said, as she hailed a cab.

They climbed in. "Au Nouveau Nez please," she told the driver.

"So, who are we impressing with this wine tonight?"

"Oh, it is not for tonight it is for Monday night. I just wanted to get it out of the way, so I could spend the rest of the weekend in my hotel. I'm an accountant and here on business. There is no reason for me to be here other than my employer thought it would be good to meet my team face to face. We are having dinner on Monday night as a team-building experience. If it was up to me, I would have flown in on Monday and out on Tuesday, but they seem to think that I needed some time to acclimate and relax. If they wanted me to relax, they should have picked a quiet little town with some hiking trails and a lake. Sorry, I do not mean to insult your city I know many people love it, but I am just not a big city guy."

"So, this is your first time in Paris, and you are going to spend the entire weekend in your room?" she asked with a disturbed look on her face.

"Yep, that's the plan, and I've now held up on my promise of telling the most uninteresting story you have ever heard," he said with a smirk on his face.

"That story is more than uninteresting it is a tragedy. There are so many wonderful things to do and see here."

"I'm sure there are but they are all big city things. Like, wait on the street to get a cab, drive to a place to wait in line, get in that place just to get rushed through so you can go back out to wait on another cab, to take you to another place to wait in line to get seated to eat, then wait on your food, then get rushed out to wait for a cab to take you back to your hotel. Doing all that by yourself and not being able to speak French doesn't sound like much fun to me. I think I will just take room service and save myself all the waiting."

"Well, now your whole weekend was just spent waiting for Monday. When you have nothing to do, then waiting for something sounds better than waiting on nothing," she said.

"Have you ever traveled by yourself? What you are saying sounds good in theory but when you get down to it, it's not as much fun as you think."

She was very confused by this person. She liked his personality even if it was a little odd, but she also felt very comfortable with him and was confident that he was not looking for a one-night affair. She could not stand the thought of someone coming to Paris and sitting in a hotel. That was just absurd to her.

He could see the frustration on her face. He had spent weeks doing his research and studying her. He knew she loved Paris and there was no way she could let anyone come here and not have a wonderful time.

"Well," she said, with a pause. She realized that she had driven halfway across Paris with a guy she did not know the name of.

"Well Steve," she said.

He interrupted her, "My name is not Steve my name is—"

But before he could get out his name, she stopped him.

"I do not care what your name is. I am not going to let

you come to my city for the first time and sit in a hotel room all weekend. If you do not want to be alone then I will be your tour guide at least for today. As for my name you can call me Shelly. Yeah, that sounds like a good name. I just don't want you to get the wrong idea of what's going on here. This is just a day of site seeing and at the end of the day, we will go our separate ways not even knowing each other's names. How does that sound?"

He smiled and said, "That sounds great. Lead the way, Shelly."

He started to think maybe this wouldn't be a total waste of a day. She seemed full of energy and excitement and not full of normal girl bullshit. He was concerned about the name change as he already knew her name was Ariane, and her dad was one of the most paranoid and largest arms dealers in all of France. Maybe that's why she didn't want him to know her name. If he didn't know her name, then he would not be able to find out about all her family's problems or get on her dad's radar. Which is kind of funny as that is exactly what he was looking to do.

As she reached forward to give the cab driver a new location, he used the opportunity to reach in her purse and take her phone. He could not have someone especially daddy calling and messing up his plans. In one quick motion, he put the phone on silent and stuffed it in the small of his back hiding it under his shirt. No longer than it took her to lean back from finishing her conversation with the cab driver the car stopped.

She hopped out of the car and said, "Pay the man Stevie."

While she was walking away, he acted like he was fumbling with his wallet, but used the spare moment to contact Chip, who was his counterpart in the mission, that he had acquired the phone and would be dropping it in a trash can within a few meters from his current location.

"Make sure you are the next person to use the trash Chip!" he said sternly.

He preferred to run missions alone, but the agency would not allow it. He didn't like relying on anyone but himself and just saw Chip as an annoyance. He never treated Chip with respect, actually he never treated anyone with respect as was evident when the cab driver said, "Excuse me?" thinking he was talking to him.

He replied saying, "None of your dam business!" and with a smirk, he gave him an almost nonexistent and insulting tip.

They spent the rest of the afternoon traveling around Paris. She had a good mix of touristy stuff like the Louvre Museum and Norte Dame mixed in with local things like street fairs and lunch on the water. She tried to take him to the Eiffel Tower, but he shut that down telling her as much as he was enjoying her company, he was not going to go stand in line to look at a monument of a giant penis. She tried to act offended but could not help but laugh the whole time.

With every minute that passed, he was transitioning himself from the shy helpless man she found in the market to a confident fun outgoing person that had her hanging on to his every word. He accomplished this so subtle that it was just before dinner when she finally realized that the power of the relationship had changed. It happened as she was looking in a mirror after using the restroom. She was teasing her hair, straightening her blouse trying to make herself as beautiful as possible, and for what? She couldn't believe she was doing this for the man that just hours ago was holding cooking wine in his hand. At that point, she started to think. Then she stopped herself.

You're having a great day. Don't over think this and ruin it like you always do. Just for once lose control and not worry about tomorrow, just let him be in control we can go back to being responsible on Monday.

With all this thought of being responsible, she just remembered that she had not called her father yet to let him know she would not make dinner with him tonight. Dam her phone was out with Steve in her purse. She would have to make the call when she got back to the table.

While she was in the bathroom, he decided to make the first contact. Chip now had her phone and was able to link his phone and hers together. He instructed Chip to make the call. The phone rang and her father seeing her number on the line answered.

"Hi, baby I thought you would be here by now."

"She will never be there again! You think you can take one of mine and I would not retaliate, you son of a bitch? Hope you liked seeing this number on your phone because it is the last time you will."

Then he hung up the call. This was going to start a fire storm in the city tonight and he would not be able to keep running around with her all night, but he felt okay with the way things were going and was sure that after dinner she would be willing to let him make the next plans.

She came back to find him staring at the bottle of wine they had ordered with dinner. She sat down and asked what he was doing as she reached in her purse for her phone.

He said, "We never got the wine for my party on

Monday. I really like this one I think I will just order a bottle to go when we leave."

At this point, she wasn't listening that close as she started to panic a little bit, tearing everything out of her purse looking everywhere for her phone. But it was not in there.

He asked her if she was okay.

She was confused because she knew she had her phone when she left the house this morning.

"I can't seem to find my phone. I need to let my father know I will not be making dinner with him tonight. He is going to be worried if I do not show up."

Steve pulled his phone out of his pocket and said to her, "Use mine to call him. I don't answer the phone when I do not know the number but maybe your dad is different. If nothing else, you can leave him a message."

She did not like the idea of her dad having her new friends' number. This was going to make her life way more complicated on Monday and she would now have to answer a bunch of questions, but she already decided in the bathroom that nothing was going to ruin this night. She made the call. Chip had already set up the phone so no matter what number she dialed it would go to a copy of her father's voice mail message. Chip set up a dummy box for this call. As she made the call, he knew her father would not answer, and she would have to leave a message.

Back in his home, Nicolas had just been hung up on. Panic started to set in. Nicolas grabbed a vase off the table and threw it against the wall.

"Tony get in here. I just got a call someone has Ariane, they called me from her cell."

"What do they want?" Tony said.

"He didn't want anything. He asked if we thought we could take one of his and he would not retaliate. What have we done lately who could this be?"

"I don't know boss you've been busy the last few months."

"He must want something! We need to get everyone out in the streets right now looking for her. Start breaking some legs 100,000 Euros to anyone with information. We will start with DeAngelo. Didn't we take out one of his guy's last week? Or maybe Tommy we had some run-ins with them last month. Let's get going!"

"Boss you can't go out there you never leave this house. Too many people want you dead. Right now, we don't know for sure what is going on. For all you know, someone grabbed her bag and just called you from her cell to get you to walk out the front door. Let me go do some checking and make sure she is not just sitting at home. I will have some boys go over to her house and look."

"No, we need to go. She was supposed to be here for dinner tonight, and she is not here something has to be wrong."

"Boss, I love her too, but we must be smart here. I will go start taking care of this myself. Just stay here until you hear from me. That way when she shows up for dinner you will be here."

Tony left and immediately got everyone looking and engaged in the situation. This was going to be a bloody night in Paris.

At the restaurant, they were just finishing up dinner. He ordered a bottle of wine to go. Then asked her what was next on the agenda. She suggested a walk down by the water.

He said, "That sounded good, but if you don't mind, I would like to stop by my hotel to drop off the wine." This was the plan the whole time. It had been almost 10 minutes since he hung up on her father, so he knew the streets were not going to be safe for them to be on for long.

She smiled and said, "Are you just trying to get me back to your room?"

He acted embarrassed and said, "No you can wait in the lobby I just don't want to carry this around all night."

She laughed as her face lit up and said, "It's okay," but he knew they would not be leaving the room once they got there for the rest of the night.

The hotel was coincidently up the street from the restaurant. She thought she had picked the restaurant, but he rarely leaves anything to chance. His subtle influences insured that they would be back at his hotel for the night within minutes of making the first contact.

They entered the hotel lobby, and here was the moment of truth. He had to give her the opportunity to wait for him downstairs while he dropped off the bottle of wine. Knowing full well this was not an option.

He said, "I will be right back down just give me a couple of minutes."

He started to pull away. There are always a few moments in a job that you cannot control, and this was one. If she said, okay, then what was the plan? He could go up and come back down sick which is another situation he could not control because then she might just go home and even if she did come up, she probably would not stay all night with someone who is sick.

If both plans fail, there's always the everything's gone

to hell plan of really kidnapping her, but that makes for an uncomfortable night of crying and awkward conversation. It would be a night of why are you doing this to me. He would much more enjoy a night of seduction to a night of tears.

Luckily, he didn't even get arm's length away before she pulled him back and said, "Don't be silly, I can come up with you."

The crisis was avoided, and he knew he was about to have a great night. They took the elevator up to his room and he asked her, "What do you do for a living?"

"I am an accountant just like you. I work mostly for my dad, keeping his books."

"So maybe my uninteresting story was not so uninteresting to you. Turns out we are both dull and boring and here you had me thinking all day that you were the queen of Paris."

She slapped his chest and laughed as they walked to his door. He put the key in his door, and they walked in. He placed the wine on the dresser. She grabbed him and threw him on the bed.

"I'll show you boring," she said.

She jumped on top of him and started taking his shirt off. He grabbed her and threw her to the side as he forced himself to be on top of her and said, "You may be the queen of Paris out there but in here, I'm the tour guide."

He slowly started unbuttoning her blouse and whispered in her ear, "Just tell me what you want, and I will help you." He kissed the side of her neck and slowly ran his hand up the back of her leg pulling down her panties, teasing her, tasting her. "Now what can I help you with."

She said, softly, "Oh you can help me?"

As she said that he slowly started to take her, and she yelled, "Yes help me, please help me! Please help me! Help me! Help me Please Help me!"

He took his time being both gentle and rough at just the right times. He had to make sure that this was not going to just be a one-time affair. He had to make sure she would want to stay all night.

As he lay there running his finger slowly down her breast, he started to realize that this was different than all the other times before. He wasn't already thinking about the next mission and was content to lay with her all night. Although she was younger, she was not immature and needy like most girls. Seducing her was extremely easy. This would usually be an annoyance for him as he loves a good challenge. But as he thought back on the day, he realized there were times of the day he just enjoyed her company and was not only thinking about the mission. As that thought went through his mind, he realized that he was here for a job and needed to get the next steps in motion.

He rolled out of bed grabbed his phone off the nightstand and excused himself to the bathroom. He locked the door and turned on the water. He put the phone to his ear and told Chip to make the second call from her phone. The phone rang, and her father answered the phone.

"Who is this? What do you want?" Nicolas asked.

He waited a few seconds then said, "You and your boys have been busy, all that manpower and still you cannot find me or her."

"What do you want?" Nicolas said again.

"I told you I do not want anything other than to make you suffer, so I am going to send you a video of her dying."

"Please no I will give you anything you want!"

"Anything?" he asked.

"Yes, anything."

"Okay I will take the 30 thousand Euros you keep in the safe in your house."

"30 thousand Euros is all you want? You took my baby girl over 30 thousand Euros!"

"Well, if you had more in your house, I would take more, but I know you have already sent Tony and all the rest of your crew out to look for Ariane and me. So that means you are by yourself, and I want it to stay that way. We all know you're a stupid old man and that Tony is the one with the brains. So if I see him or anyone else come to your house or if you leave your house with anyone, she dies. You will bring the 30 thousand to the front of the Maison Souquet Hotel. There is a fountain there, you will stand in front of it and wait for me. If you are not alone or it takes you more than 20 minutes to get here, I will kill her."

"How do I know you have her? I am not doing anything until I talk to her."

"Okay, you want me to make her talk to you here she is," he said.

There was about a 30-second pause on the phone then her father heard his daughter's voice saying, "Please help me! Please help me! Help me! Help me Please Help me!"

He came back on the phone and said, "20 minutes."

Her father asked, "How do I know you will not just kill us both?"

"I probably will, and you don't. You can do nothing and receive a video and live with that image the rest of your life or you can be a father and bring the money alone to the hotel and hope I am a man of my word." He hung up the phone.

"Okay Chip we are on. Ring my phone when he is close."

He washed his hands in the sink then unlocked the door and came back out to lay with her. She kissed him and said, "What's next tour guide?"

"Just let me know what you want, I am here to be helpful and to please."

"Yes, you most certainly are," she said as she gave him another kiss.

"So, do you still think it would be appalling to spend all weekend in a hotel room? Because that may be just what we are going to do."

"Well, you did just put up a convincing argument, but I am not sure I can let you get your way. I may need a little more convincing to see things your way."

"I think I can do that. How about I go down and get us some coffee and a midnight snack. You can freshen up, and we can see if I can convince you some more."

"How about you start convincing me now and we call room service."

"Once we start this, I do not want to be disturbed I think you can wait a few minutes for me."

"Okay but don't be long."

He put on his pants grabbed a jacket and a room key and said, "I won't be long." He went to the elevator and took it down to the second floor to another room he had in the hotel. This was a room that had the best view of the fountain out front. He made sure the do not disturb sign was still on the door as he entered. Everything was setup. He already had the rifle assembled and ready to go. He hid it in the couch just in case the maid did not respect the do not disturb sign. It has been 17 minutes since the second call. He opened the double doors to the balcony then checked the silencer on the rifle and laid down in the prone position to get ready for the shot. He pulled out his cell phone.

"Chip, are we good to go?" he asked.

"Yes, Nicolas has left the house alone as instructed. He has just parked and is walking toward the fountain now."

"Okay, I see him."

Nicolas looked frantic. His coat buttons were even buttoned in the wrong order. Walking short distances made him short of breath. This was probably the furthest the fat guy had walked in 10 years. Nicolas reached the fountain.

"Call him Chip."

Nicolas answered his phone right away. "I have the money and I am alone what do you want me to do now."

"Face the hotel and look at the second-story window."

Nicolas turned around and looked. "Okay, what now."

"Now I want you to die," he said, as he squeezed the trigger. The bullet found its mark right between Nicolas's eyes.

Chip came on the phone. "Nice work. The mission is complete. Now go to the rendezvous point so we can head home."

"The mission is not complete there is still one loose end," he said.

"No. She is not a loose end, and she was not part of the mission. I heard the way you talked to her you never talk to anyone like that she can live. Please just let her live," Chip pleaded.

He hung up the phone on Chip and grabbed a 9mm that was in one of the cases he had in the room. He walked out the door and took the stairs up, he could not have chip stopping the elevator. He used his key to open the door. He swung the door open as far as it would go. He liked to use the slamming of the door to mask the shot. He entered the room. She was on the phone with a scared look on her face. Chip had tried to warn her to get out, but Chip was too late. As the DOOR SLAMMED SHUT, he squeezed the trigger. BANG! The bullet had again found its mark right between her eyes. He walked over to the phone next to the bed and picked it up.

"Why would you do that Chip! Why did you make her die scared! She could have died happy not knowing anything but instead her last moments were fear. I did not want that for her, but that is on you not me. You must live with that now."

"Screw you she didn't have to die at all!" Chip yelled.

"I just saved her the anxiety of losing her father," he said.

"You're getting more and more out of control. Get back to the meeting place," Chip said.

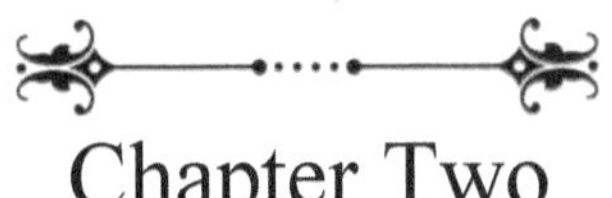

Chapter Two
Back Home

"Niles, wake up. You are having another nightmare," Nicole said.

Niles woke up covered in sweat his heart was racing.

"What were you dreaming about?" Nicole said.

She knew this was a worthless question because Niles could never answer her. Niles never remembers his dreams, but she still asked in the hopes that this would be the first time.

"I don't know, I can't remember. Did I say anything?"

"No, but you are scared of everything so for all I know you could be dreaming about the spider you ran away from in the living room last week. Remember the one you made me kill." she laughed as she pulled him close to her to calm him down.

"It's over now. Let's go back to sleep."

Niles lay in her arms and was frustrated that this happened again but was thankful she was there.

"I don't know what I would do without you Nicole."

"Well, we know you would live with a lot more spiders, that's for sure," she said jokingly.

"Let's go back to sleep"

Niles was already in her arms and didn't want to let this moment slip away. They were both awake and the kids were sound asleep. They did not have too many moments with just them, so Niles slowly started kissing her neck. She did her best to return his affection, but knew his stamina was not the best and they would both be left disappointed again. Him for not being able to please his wife, and her for being left wanting more.

"Sorry you are just too sexy. I can't control myself," Niles said, to lighten the moment.

"I know honey and that is what I love about you now let's get some sleep."

They woke up the next morning to the same routine as every day. Nile's jumped in the shower while Nicole made the kids breakfast. Then Niles would make his way down and they would eat together as a family. Then Niles would take the kids to school. If it was Monday Niles would have to take his and their elderly neighbors' trash to the sidewalk. Tuesday Niles would only have to take Ms. Gonzales's trash to the sidewalk. She used a different service, so it was on a different day.

Niles would help all the people in the neighborhood in one way or another especially the elderly. The rest of the week would consist of driving the kids to school then driving himself to his job. At his job, Niles would walk through the front door every morning and go see each of the other two coworkers in the building. Greeting them politely asking them how their night or weekend was. Then asked them if everything was okay before walking in the back room to go get his coffee, before starting his day's work. Niles worked 8:00 am to 4:00 pm Monday through Friday, picking the kids up from school after work before heading home.

At home, Niles would make time to play with the

kids or help them with their homework. Nicole would have dinner ready to go at around 6:00 pm. They always tried to eat as a family. There would be times when the kid's sports or dance lesson would push out dinner, but other than that they were a very well-rounded and happy family. Niles and Nicole would spend the weekends with friends if the kids did not have a sports activity. They were the hostess and the planners of their network of friends and their house is the spot that everyone would hang out at.

Thursday started the same as every Thursday. Niles showered, had breakfast, and dropped the kids off at school, but when Niles got to work the parking lot was full and a car was in his spot. Niles is never one for confrontation, so Niles left the parking lot.

Niles decided to use the opportunity to get bagels for himself and his coworkers. The bagel shop was just two blocks down the road and their parking lot was never full. Niles knew the owner well as getting bagels for his coworkers was a regular occurrence. Niles was sure she would not mind if his car was left there for just one day. Niles got the bagels and was walking back to work when a loud noise rang in his ears. A brick next to him exploded. His mind could not process what was going on. Another loud noise and another brick exploded. Niles slowly started to look around and could see in the reflection of the glass of the store window a man running up to him. He tackled Niles pushing him down next to a large truck. "Saying what the hell is wrong with you?"

More shots were hitting the building next to them, but they were now covered by the truck.

"Do you not know what gun shots sound like? They are shooting at me not you but how can you be so stupid as to not get down when you hear gunshots." The man was extremely angry. He didn't even seem scared for his own life. He just seemed angry that Niles did not take cover.

"I am going to run north. I suggest you run south in the opposite direction of me. Or just stay here and die I don't give a shit." The man said as he took off running north. He was fast. One more gunshot went off then the man disappeared behind the building, and he was gone. The shooting stopped but Niles sat there for another 10 minutes before moving. His mind could still not comprehend what just happened. One of his coworkers came out and helped Niles into the front door of their office.

"Are you okay are you shot?" his coworker asked.

"No, I am okay. I think I just need to call my wife," Then Niles picked up the phone on the desk and dialed his wife's number.

She picked up. "Hello?" She sounded out of breath.

"What are you doing?" Niles asked.

"Just working out. Aren't you at work? What's going on?"

"I was walking in to work when gunshots started hitting all around me. I am okay but I just needed to hear your voice."

"Niles are you sure you're okay?" she asked with concern.

"Yes, I am okay. Like I said, I just needed to hear your voice."

"Okay, can I talk to one of your coworkers just to make sure you are not in shock?"

Niles handed over the phone, "Can you please tell my wife I'm okay?"

His coworker got on the phone with Nicole. Niles could hear his coworker and wife talking but could not make out what they were saying. Niles heard him say "Yes, he is physically okay." Then his coworker handed the phone back to Niles.

"If you're okay, I think the best thing for you to do is get your cup of coffee and start your day at work. Honey, I do not want to seem insensitive, but it is over. Please do not let this destroy you. I know you may think this is a big deal, but I promise you we will get through it and I think the fastest way to do that is to get back to normal. You can come home now if you want, and we can talk about it. "Nicole said.

"No honey, I think you are right. We can talk about it tonight. I love you and your right it is over. I will see you tonight," Niles said then hung up the phone. Niles immediately started to feel better. "I think I need a cup of coffee," Niles told his coworkers, then walked to the back room.

Not far away the back door slammed. He came in furious. He looked at Chip. "Can you believe that guy just standing there not moving at all. How the hell did he not get shot? That's one lucky asshole." He looked at Chip again and shouted, "And what the hell were you doing during all this? Thanks for the help! You better at least have a location on the shooter."

Chip said, "I know you won't, but you should calm down your handler has already neutralized the situation and the shooter is down.

"How the hell do they know who I am, get that bitch on the phone and let me talk to her," he said.

Chip picked up the phone and called the handler. This was the person responsible for them when not in an active mission. The company had many divisions some were in active mission-critical, and others were off active mission-critical. None of them ever knew anything about the other.

Chip said, "He wants to talk to you" then handed the phone over.

He started yelling at her immediately. "You're doing a dam fine job of looking out for me. You have one dam job how hard can that be."

She said, "From your asshole tone it doesn't sound like you are dead, so it looks like I am still doing a dam fine job."

"Who the hell was shooting at me?"

"I am not sure yet, but my team has the shooter down across the street from you. Unfortunately, we could not bring him down alive so that will make the job a little harder, but we will figure it out."

"He started yelling at her again. What building is it? I'm on my way! This needs to be done right!"

She yelled back, "You will do no such thing. This is my job to resolve. Your job is to get ready for the next mission and unless you want me to pull you off that mission then I suggest that is what you should start doing right now." Then she hung up on him.

"Incompetent bitch," he said, as he hung up the phone. He looked at Chip and said, "What are you looking at? Let's get back to work planning the mission."

They started planning and working out the details of the next mission, but he could not get his mind off that guy. Finally, he told Chip, "I'm taking a break and getting out of here for a while. Keep working on this and I will be back soon."

Chip begged him, "Please listen to her and just drop it. They will handle this we have too much time already on this mission to be pulled from it."

"I am not going to look for the shooter. I just need to clear my head," he said, as he left and walked down to the bagel shop. He could remember the guy was holding bagels and they must have come from that shop. He walked in and said, "Excuse me, ma'am, I am sure you heard all the commotion coming from down the street earlier."

She said, "Yes do you know what was going on? Did they find the person shooting the gun?"

He said, "I do not know anything about that, but while that was going on there was a man about my height with a beard. He was caring bagels I think from this shop. He helped me out a little during all that and I would like to thank him. I know you must have a lot of customers but by chance do you happen to know him."

"Oh you must be talking about Niles. Niles is very friendly and would help anyone. That is his red car right out there. Someone took his parking spot today, so Niles had to park there. You could leave him a note on it or wait around for him to come back if you want."

"Thank you very much ma'am I will do that and thank you for your time," he said, as he left. He got the number of the license plate. He could find out all his information from that. Eventually, he would want to meet him again but for now, he could just do some research on him.

He went back to the office to look up the license plate. Chip was trying to pull him away to plan the mission. Chip did not want him getting his mind set on another objective. He had a one-track mind and if it was focused on the mission, that was great, but when his focus was moved off the mission then all plans for the mission would stop. He got the home address of the owner of the car. He was not quite sure what he was going to do with that information, but he was content to move on and go back to planning the mission. Besides he was getting tired of listening to Chip's bitching.

The two worked the rest of the day then he went out the back door as always to go home. Tonight, would be different. This could be the first night in a while he did not continue to plan the mission. He still could not get his mind off Niles.

On the other side, Niles did exactly the opposite. Niles listened to his wife and put himself fully into his work until it was time for him to go home. Niles worked the full day. Then walked out the front door like always to go pick up the kids and take them home to his wife. At home, Nicole was extremely surprised the night went just like every other night. She was expecting Niles to be a basket case, but they put the kids to bed just like every other night, then they went to bed themselves.

In bed, Nicole asked Niles to talk about what happened to him that day, but Niles said, "I am fine I just want to move on as you said. There is no need to dwell on it, let's just go to bed."

Nicole was not sure if she fully believed this would be the end of it but was at peace with letting it go for now and getting some sleep.

The next morning was normal for Niles. The kids

got to school, Niles got to work, and his parking spot was open. Niles parked the car. Went to work and had his normal morning conversation with his coworkers. Then went to the back room to get his coffee.

Chip however did not get the same response. The normal asshole that usually came in from the back door was much quieter. He just came in sat down and started going to work. Chip could tell his mind was not fully on his work, but Chip was glad to pick up the slack so long as he did not have to put up with any attitude. They made it until about lunch when he told Chip, "I'm going out to lunch today."

"You know you can't leave the office during the workday," Chip protested. But it was too late he was out the door hailing down a cab. He gave the cab driver the address he got off the license plate.

The cab pulled up in front of the house. "Your total is $42 dollars."

"Just keep the meter running I won't be long and will need a ride back."

"Okay, no problem," the cab driver said.

He walked up to the door and rang the doorbell. Nicole answered the door with a confused look on her face. "Can I help you?"

"Is Niles here?" he asked.

"No, he is at work. Is there something I can help you with?"

"Of course, that would make sense. I swear ever since that incident yesterday I cannot get my head clear. What type of man does not make any attempt to save himself?" he questioned out loud.

"Wait, are you here to try and talk to Niles about what happened yesterday? You can never do that.

Niles is a fragile man, and for some reason is handling this very well. Please if you need to know anything about Niles, I can talk to you. But I do not want him to ever relive or think about yesterday again. Here is my number if you need to talk about it, but please stay far away from Niles and never try to contact him again. I told Niles to just go do his work and forget about yesterday. That seems to be working for him and I would suggest you go and do the same."

"Yes, ma'am, sorry for bothering you," he said as he turned and walked away.

He went back to the cab and the driver took him back to the office. He walked through the door and sat down at his desk.

Chip came over and said, "She wants to talk to you."

He said, "Shut the hell up. I'm not going to call her. She can walk her ass down here if she wants to talk to me or she can fire me but other than that I have nothing to say to that bitch."

He was talking about his non-interactive control off-leave engagement. The organization likes to keep separation for mission departments. They classify everything as off-leave or off-mission or on-leave or on-mission. Missions' controllers are different people for each one. They never meet in person always on the phone and no one ever knows any person's real name.

The next few days at work he was stilled distracted but at least able to run through different scenarios for the next mission. Now his mind was not as much on Niles, but he found himself thinking a lot about Nicole. At lunch that day he could not resist it anymore. He picked up the phone and called the number she had given him. Nicole answered. "Hello?"

"Hi, it's me the man that came to your house a few days back. Sorry, I won't take much of your time, but I want to take you up on your offer to tell me about Niles. I cannot get him or you for that matter off my mind. How can you live with someone so weak?" he asked.

"Niles may be scared of everything. Which at times can cause him mental anxiety, but Niles is not weak. The love Niles gives to me, and his children outweigh all the weaknesses you see."

"But a guy like that will never be able to protect you."

Nicole laughed out loud. "What would we need protecting from? It sounds like you live in a world much different from mine if you think we need protection."

He didn't know how to respond to that comment, so he said, "Thank you for your time. I won't bother you again."

"That's okay, you sound like you may need someone to talk to from time to time if you do, please feel free to call me again, we can talk about anything."

"Thank you," he said and hung up the phone.

Over the course of the next few weeks, he found himself calling Nicole more and more. At first, he would ask more questions about Niles, but then it just turned to normal everyday conversation. He found himself telling her things he should not be telling her. Things about work and his job. Things he knew upper management would not like, but for some reason, he did not care.

Chapter Three
Begin the First Missions

One day while they were talking, Nicole asked about his first mission and how he got started in his business.

It was about 10 years ago. There were a lot of high-profile people dying and some of them from our agency. They were random kills that affected many different organizations. We eventually concluded that it was just a pay-for-hire assassin that was very clever and good at his job. Once they came to this conclusion, they open the *Number One Assassin* or NOA task force for short.

It took some time, but the agency eventually found NOA was using a small-time very cheap underground group of assassin's job board to get his assignments. Normally this job board was just used for small-time hits like cheating girlfriends or abusive husbands.

This was how NOA was able to stay under the radar for so long. No top-level agency would ever spend any time looking at these small-time crimes. They would be handled by local PD, and local PD would not be informed of the high-profile crimes so they would not be able to match them to information they may receive from criminals they would catch from the association.

NOA never used the same method to kill his victims. Not even the small-time criminals that ran the assassin board were aware of what was going on. They would receive a small fee for allowing NOA to use their job board. Then NOA would give instructions on how to pay him directly outside their network. It was a brilliant setup. It wasn't until after we realized how NOA was getting his jobs that we discreetly infiltrated the small-time criminal's organization. With this information, we could go back and look at their completed jobs.

That's when we realized over half his jobs were thought to be accidents. If it wasn't for the number of accidents that accumulated in a short time frame to high profile people, NOA would probably still be working today.

It was just dumb luck how the agency found out about NOA. It was the first time we know of that NOA made a mistake. James was the CEO of one of the lethal neurotoxins manufacturers that our agents use, and good friends with our head director. James had an apartment that was off books that no one knew about. A place for him to be by himself away from his family.

One day James went there and found his mistress dead on the floor. James could tell from her body that she was killed by the same neurotoxins that his company made. Before calling the police, James called our agency to handle the investigation. It was only because of his friendship with our director that our agency even decided to look at this in the first place. James had never given anyone a key before her. The neurotoxin was released from a canister that was activated when the front door was opened.

Our first thought was that James was the target. So, we looked at all James associates and competitors for a motive. Was it someone who wanted his job or a competitor that wanted him out of the way?

We could never find a motive or evidence that linked anyone to the crime. Then one of the team members approached it from a different angle. Maybe she was the actual target and not him. They traced her phone records and listened to her voice mails. They found some angry messages from a guy she was sleeping with at the same time as James. This guy saw her with James and must have just lost it from the messages he was leaving her. Our team did some investigation on the guy, but it did not seem like he would have the resources to kill her this way. The neurotoxins she was killed with would not be easy to come by. Either there had to be some help from a professional or there was still a large part of the puzzle they were missing.

This is what led our team to start looking at small-time amateur hit men. We found a few organizations that for a small fee were willing to let us look at the last few months of their jobs that went out for hire. The problem was none of them were women, but after putting a few different lists together the pattern came out.

There was a list of jobs that were open for just a couple of hours and then disappeared. Most of the assassins took them for retracted jobs. It would be extremely hard to research a person, make a safe plan, and then find the person in that short amount of time.

The way it worked was a job stayed open until the person is assassinated. Then once the job is done the assassin claims the job with proof of death. Only then is the assassin paid and the job closed. The other assassins didn't discover the jobs because the jobs would close before they even started looking into them. But as we put the entire list together, the names always started with the name John for jobs that were closed within two hours.

There also was a John James that was open and closed two weeks ago. This was too big a coincidence not to be the James we were working with, but all our doubts were put to rest the next day when James was found dead in his car. The assassin put a vial of the neurotoxins in the heater core fan of James' car. When James turned on his heater, the vial was crushed by the fan, and the gas was released into the car. It all happened so fast James didn't even have time to put the car in reverse. James was found dead in his parking spot with the engine still running. When we went to look at the camera footage of the parking garage all the cameras were disabled 24 hours before the death of James. So, we were still left with no leads on the assassin. But now that we knew the process we could start coming up with a plan. That is where I came in. I was not part of the organization at all. Because some of the targets the assassin killed were in our company there were concerns the assassin or someone associated with him was in our company. The top three chairmen in the company took it upon themselves to find an agent.

How they found me or why they even came to me, to this day I do not know. I had no prior military background. Hell, I barely ever held a gun. My best guess has always been that somehow, they knew that I had no one in my life that would give a shit if I went missing, and other than my nightly whisky there wasn't anything else I was living for.

When they came to me that night, they knew everything about me and did not sugarcoat anything. They let me know I was a piece of shit and would always be one if I did not take the opportunity they were presenting me with. I was a little tuned up at the time but everything they were saying sounded good, so I said, what the hell I'm in. I assumed saying that meant I would still have the night to think about it but that wasn't the case.

As soon as I said I was in they paid my tab and said let's go. They took me to my apartment. I gather some of my clothes and that was it. We were on a plane that night to a new secret training facility. That was the last time I saw that apartment.

They flew me to a small training facility. Well, they called it a training facility.

Most of the equipment was fresh out of the box and the building looked like it had been abandoned for years. I was hoping for some time to work off my hangover the next morning, but DICH had different ideas. DICH was not his real name it stood for "Drill Instructor Central Handler." No one in the company ever knew anyone's real name and rather than giving everyone fake names, they came up with name designations based on the job they did. Eventually, I think just to piss me off, all the names became about how they handled me. DICH and CHIP, "Central Handler Intelligence Personal", were there day one with me.

The first few hours of the day we did PT. We followed that up with some spy training, but my training wasn't like what I would suspect normal spy training would be like. I had to have an accelerated timeline. In the afternoon I would start doing research and mission planning on the missions we were trying to run. I didn't get any fake training missions to fail. I had to live and learn on the fly with no room for errors.

We knew we had to look for jobs on the assassin job board that started with the name John and were closed in under two hours, but all this gave us was the first name. We had all the past names and tried to compile a list of future victims, but they were so random we couldn't find a pattern.

At first, all we could do was match the "John's" name to the dead body once it turned up. We also had to be careful how we collected evidence. We didn't want NOA to find out we were on to him. We had to let local PD run the crime scene. If we thought NOA made a mistake I would impersonate local PD to try and find some good evidence but that never happened. We only found what NOA wanted us to find.

Then one afternoon a job opened on the board with the name of John Philip. We had no Philips on our radar, and I was tired of always being one step behind, so I told Chip let's get ahead of this guy. Accept the job and close it. About thirty minutes later we got a response that said no details received please resend. "Dammit Chip another roadblock," I said.

"How the hell can we reply when we do not know who the job is for? Well, we need to reply with something Chip."

So, Chip replied with the job completed at 2:15 pm. We never got another response and about one hour later the same job with the name of John Philip opened back up. This time it was closed within minutes. This lets us know that our response was not correct, but it did put us one step closer. Now that we knew there was a response to the job, we had Chip go put a network tap on all communication from the job board. We would now be able to see the response of the next job.

I continued my training and we continued to watch for dead people with the name of Philip. Management was not happy with me jumping the gun by accepting the job without their permission. It had been two weeks and no new job had come on the board. There was a Philip that died of a heart attack, but it did not fit the style of NOA. It was a person without a position of any power and management was concerned that NOA killed Philip in a low-profile way and was now going to find a new way to accept jobs. If that was the case, we would have to start all over from scratch, and with a person as smart as NOA we may never find that trail again.

Luckily this was not the case. We never did find out if the heart attack Philip was the Philip on the job board, but about three weeks later a new job was put on the board with the name John Henry. It was accepted within one hour but this time we were able to see the reply. The reply was not the details of death but the details of the contract. It had the price of the job, $450,000 USD, and an e-mail to send the full details of the person if they wanted to accept the price of the job.

NOA was not cheap that price was triple the cost of a normal job and double the price of a high-profile job. We were really excited at first. We now had the e-mail address of NOA. Of course, it was not a Gmail or Hotmail address. NOA was too smart for that, but we felt we would still be able to track down the server of the e-mail address and eventually find his IP address off that.

Chip did find the server, but it was a temporary exchange server set up on an Amazon cloud server. This was only in-service for the time it took to get his information from the client. NOA went through the hassle of setting up new cloud exchange servers for every job. Then terminating them immediately after receiving the information. This was another setback but, from the information from the network tap Chip put on the job board we also had the IP and MAC address of the computer NOA and the person placing the order used to look at the web page on the job board.

This should have been enough information to lead us to their location, but both turned out to be newly purchased computers that accessed the job board from public places. They both accessed the WIFI from outside the location so they could not be seen by the cameras. The computers never showed back up on any network again to be traced. So, we assumed they were destroyed after the initial communication. We knew within the short time frame we had to track down all the IP addresses and locations we would never be able to find him or the purchaser. We had to assume that the initial email had information with other e-mail addresses and for all, we knew NOA was so paranoid that he also set up a temporary exchange server for that transaction as well. We would never be able to digitally catch NOA. Our only option was to play on his ego.

We gave him the name "Number One Assassin" without even knowing him. We had to hope that was truly how NOA thought of himself. There were two sides to this. The assassin side, "NOA" and the contract side. The people placing the orders and NOA accepting the order. Now we knew the process. We could easily intercept the next few orders to stop NOA from getting them, but NOA had this setup in a way that if we did that, we would never catch him. We also had no way of knowing how the sellers were learning about how to place the order. At this point, we decided not to care about the business side. Catching NOA was more important than shutting down the business side. That would be easy to shut down after catching NOA now that we knew the process.

We spent the next few weeks discussing different plans and ideas of how to get NOA to show himself without scaring him off. During that time "Henry" a CEO who had a hobby of flying solo engine planes and was an experienced pilot flew into the side of a mountain.

Chip watched the next few jobs come in and tried to track him down but was never fast enough to find him. By the time we got to the location of the IP address NOA would be gone and the computer no longer online. Our only plan was to use NOA's system against him. We knew the customers had no way of knowing who NOA was, so we decided we were just going to start taking all his jobs until we pissed him off enough to confront us. We were going to act like a rival assassin that found out about his system and start taking work from him. The training was now over. Time to get to work.

Chapter Four
First Mission 1.0

The next name that came on the list was John Robert. We had Chip accept the job, close it, and email out the price with an alternate e-mail address to complete the transaction. They sent us back a full description of Robert with instructions. They wanted the hit to look like an accident. No payment if any suspicion of foul play. Robert was a lawyer for a large firm that held many high-profile clients of large companies. After some research, we found some of his clients were former NOA victims. This made it even harder to tell if all NOA victims were related or if his clients were using NOA to clean up their business.

Chip was not keen on the idea of killing the victims on the board. With the new e-mail address and communication with the seller, Chip felt it would be easy to track down the client from the new email used to send us the documentation on Robert. Chip wanted to try and take down the whole operation from the other side, but management decided it would be too risky. NOA was the priority and if word got out at all that the board was compromised, they feared we would lose him forever.

We had to stick with the plan. Robert had to die. In all reality if we never found the message board in the first place. Robert would die by NOA. The only way to catch him was to act just like him. So, until we caught NOA if your name ended up on the message board you were going to die.

Looking back at the way NOA killed his accident victims we didn't want to just do the boring old car accident or choking accident. NOA always had a flare to his killings so if we wanted to get his attention, we wanted to do the same.

Robert worked in an office in downtown Denver. Luckily there was some WeWork office space in the office across the street from him. We rented it for the week and set up shop right across the street from him. We didn't know if NOA knew about Robert. NOA could still have a contract for Robert. This was the first time we took the contract from him so for all we knew there may have been two contracts out for Robert. It would be easy to watch for people stalking Robert then just kill them after they killed Robert. I decided from the beginning we would have to work just like NOA and leave no trace that we were ever around Robert.

Using the WeWork office was a little risky. It would be most likely what NOA would do as well, but enough regular people were using the offices every day that if we setup some actual WebEx meetings and used the facility like a normal remote office worker it would be extremely hard to tell us from all the other workers even after the job was done.

We arrived at 7:00 am in the morning and set up the WeWork office as normal office workers would. One of us always keeping an eye across the street. Robert showed up at the office at 9:00 am, arriving from the light rail on 16th Street that was just one block from his office. I liked that Robert didn't drive to work. This was going to give me more avenues to make this look like an accident. We couldn't see into his office. The first day was going to be getting an idea of his schedule. Robert came out of his office at 11:00 am for lunch, but instead of hailing a cab, Robert paid for a scooter to take him to lunch. I went outside to watch him go as far as I could before losing him. I didn't want to tail him if NOA was watching but I also wanted to see if anyone else seemed interested in him. I watched him take a right, ride down the street, stop for the light rail, and wait for it to go by before riding off to lunch. Watching the light rail go by gave me the perfect plan.

I went back into the office and had Chip pull up the schematics of the scooter Robert was riding on to lunch. My plan was to put in a remote sensor that we could activate to engage the motor while at the same time stopping the breaks from engaging. I hoped to push him right in front of the light rail hopefully destroying the scooter to the point no one would know it was tampered with.

The motor and brake cable were side by side. This made the design simple. We just had to put a remote switch on a spring-loaded rod that when triggered would open up, stopping the throttle cable from releasing and not letting the brake cable engage. We could just loosely tape the device to the bottom of the scooter so hopefully, the device would fall off and be destroyed by the light rail. We spent the rest of the afternoon tweaking the design and getting the parts we needed.

That night we rented a scooter and made the modifications. Of course, I was the one that had to test it. We took it to the park late at night, I jumped on and road it down the sidewalk about 10 feet and Chip triggered the device. I accelerated through the grass heading right for a tree. I tried to do the jump and run trick, but it didn't work I just ended up sliding face first in the grass. The design worked great except the scooter did not stop. It bounced off the tree and kept running until it hit some bushes. Once the pin was engaged to the motor and the break was stuck open the pin would not come out.

It was a good thing we tested it or else the tires would have been spinning and spinning after Robert was hit by the light rail. That would have been a dead giveaway that the scooter was rigged. This was an easy solution to fix. We just had to make the switch so it would expand then contract. This also solved the problem of removing the device from the scooter. We could lightly tape the device with a beveled edge that would pull itself off the scooter when engaged. Then it would just fall off on the street when we disengaged it. We ran another test which went much better. This time I did not have to jump off because Chip could just disengage the device.

The next morning, we went back into the office across the street from Robert's office. Around 10:30 am I went down the street and gave some kids a few prepaid visa cards. I told them I was from the scooter company, and I was giving away free rides for the day. I needed to make sure that our scooter was the only one there Robert could choose. After all the scooters were gone. I gave another teenager our scooter and told her that if she would take this scooter and leave it in front of Robert's building, I would give her a Visa card for future rides. She did what I asked, and it worked perfectly. Robert came out of the office right at 11:00 am and got on the scooter. The only problem was Robert didn't go right. This time Robert went left. I got to watch him go by me in the wrong direction. Robert went to lunch and came back which would not have been a big deal except for the fact that Robert didn't come back on the same scooter. Since we were not following him, we had no clue where our scooter was. This was the first time I learned that you always need to have a backup plan. Chip spent that afternoon building another device on a new scooter.

We let the WeWork office go the next day. We knew his routine and did not have to watch him come to work anymore. Around 10:30 am the next day I repeated the same dog and pony show with the prepaid Visa card to get only one scooter in front of the office. I waited patiently for him to come out. It was 11:00 am and no Robert. At 11:05 am the scooter was rented by another pedestrian. I had Chip follow him, so we didn't lose another scooter. Robert eventually came out at 11:20 am. There were no scooters in front of the office so Robert had to walk down the street for lunch.

That night I spent a lot of time coming up with other plans. If this plan did not come together on day three, I was going to have to take the risk of following him home on the train and finding another plan. There are only so many days you can act like a scooter salesman in the same area before you arouse suspicions. On day three I followed the same routine as the two days before. I had a returning customer for the free ride which I did not like but they already knew what was going on, so I figured I would give them another free ride.

I got our scooter in front of Robert's office and lo and behold today Robert was on time. Today I was filled with a lot of emotion as I watched him get on the scooter. Robert was taking more time than usual to get on the scooter. Was it going to be another failed attempt? Robert had to hurry if he was going to meet the train at the right moment. Finally, the scooter was on its way and headed in the right direction. I wasn't sure if Chip was going to engage the device or not. This was going to be close. "Now Chip, now! Do it! Do it," I silently said to myself.

Chip did engage the scooter, and I could not believe my eyes our plan worked. Robert was pushed in front of the light rail and died instantly. The light rail came to a screeching halt and people started running to help Robert. I could see there was no way to survive the impact. The train drug him over 600 feet before it stopped, and blood was all over the place. My first thought was to go pick up Chip's device off the ground, but cell phones were filming everywhere. I could see the device fell before the tracks and the scooter was pushed up the track with Robert, so I decided to leave it and have someone other than Chip or I come to get it later that night.

My next thoughts were random. You would think I would be happier after two failed attempts. We had finally completed our mission, but then my thoughts went to, did I just kill a man. Well, actually Chip did. His finger activated the device, but it was my plan. NOA would have killed him anyway. I could have warned him but then more people would die. At that moment I was neither happy nor sad. More confused I would say. Then I just decided this was stupid. I already signed up for this life and in this job, there could be no emotions. People were going to die I had to either be okay with it or quit, and there wasn't going to be any quit from me. Not until either me or NOA were dead.

We flew back to the office that night. Chip sent the proof of death, and we were paid our commission within ten minutes. I figured it would be fast but not ten minutes fast, but the more I thought about it when you're paying for top-level assassins you probably do not want to get on the wrong side of someone like that.

Chapter Five
First Mission 1.1

W e had to wait about two weeks before the next job came in. I was glad it was Chip and not me that had to stare at the job board all day. When the job finally came in, Chip was on top of it and accepted our next job. It was for John Isabel. "Hmm, Isabel?" I thought. This is most likely going to be a woman. I just got over a self-reflection at the end of the last job and said if I signed up for this life and this job there could be no emotions, but did I want to be a guy that killed women and children?

Throughout this whole process, it never crossed my mind. All the previous people were men, and most of them were shitty men at that. My first instinct was the same as before. Screw it. It's the job. Let's move on, but this time it was not going to be as easy to move on. I made Chip upped the price on this job by $100,000 USD. From $450,000 USD to $550,000 USD. If the bastard was going to make me kill a woman, it made me feel better that it was going to cost them more to do it. Chip did the email exchange, and it was a woman.

Isabela was a pharmaceutical chemist for a very large company. Not only was she a woman but in my mind, she was probably an innocent woman that was going to cost the company money, and they needed her silenced.

This job was in Virginia. The client had given us her address. I told Chip we had to do much better planning for this one. There could be no more options for her to turn right or left. This plan had to be solid. Chip agreed the plan had to be solid but explained to me that coming up with the plan was going to be easy. The customer had already given us detailed instructions on how they wanted her killed. Isabel lived with her sister and the client wanted us to make it look like her sister killed her. They wanted her sister to go to prison for the murder. Chip must have seen a disturbed look on my face.

"Hey, it's a job. Don't take it personally," Chip said.

You would think with all the internal conflict I was having with killing people and now knowing I had to kill a woman and destroy her sister's life that this news would have been what was disturbing me. It was, but not for the reasons it should have. I was finding myself a little angry that I didn't get to come up with the plan. Hell, the customer even gave us the location of the bar the sister went to on Friday nights.

In the last job coming up with the plan and tweaking all the details of the plan was exhilarating to me. Not to mention it also kept my mind occupied. I was not going to be able to work on fine-tuning the plan to perfection this time. This mission was already laid out. I would just have a few small improvisations to come up with on the fly.

We flew to Virginia rented a car and drove by Isabel's house. We parked up the street but only stayed for ten minutes. We didn't want to raise any suspicions and we already knew the sister would be at the bar later that night.

The next stop was the bar. I wanted to get there early and scope the place out. I thought Chip would have to disable a security system but to our surprise, there wasn't one. It was a small country bar. The dance floor took up most of the bar. Line dancing was the reason Isabel's sister went there. From the picture we got of her she was not an attractive woman, so I assumed line dancing is all she ever did. Not too many guys would probably be hitting on her.

I went into the bar about twenty minutes before she was supposed to be there. I sat down at the bar and ordered a drink. It had been a while since a drink had touched my lips. I wasn't anticipating that it would be a problem for me, but man did that first beer taste good. I had two beers down before I knew it. The old times came back to me in an instant and it was like I never left.

This place was starting to feel like home again. After the second beer, I snapped back out of it. I held off drinking the third one until Isabel's sister arrived. The bar top was small so she would have no choice but to sit by me. She came in and sat at the bar and ordered herself a drink.

I wanted to ignore her at first. This seemed to be the treatment she was used to. She just sat there drinking her drink by herself. After I finished my third beer, I asked her how her night was going.

She kind of looked around as if to see if I was talking to someone else. It took a few seconds but when she realized I wasn't, she said, "Good, how is your night?"

I said, "Better now that I have someone to talk to."

We introduced ourselves to each other and continued with a small awkward conversation. She told me she was here to line dance, but the bar only played line dancing songs at the top of each hour. The rest of the time was for regular couples dancing. I tried my best to keep the conversation moving until the line dancing started but it was not easy. She was a very strange woman. She had a nervous laugh after every sentence. She laughed even if the sentence was not meant to be funny.

When the first line dancing song came on, she didn't get up and go out on the dance floor. I asked her, "Aren't you here to line dance. Please don't let me stop you from going out there."

She said she was enjoying our conversation and would like to continue with it rather than dance. I made a promise to her that I would still be here when the songs were over.

"Besides I am looking forward to seeing how good you are out there."

She smiled and said, "Okay," grabbed her drink, and went out on the floor.

I was hoping she was going to leave her drink with me, but I guess even ugly girls are still trained not to let their drink out of their sight. This was easily overcome by just ordering her one more drink while she was gone.

She was still on the dance floor when the drink came. This made it easy for me to add a shot of vodka to it. I needed her to be visibly drunk on the security camera in her front yard. I thought that would be a good way to help her get there a little faster.

I was not sure if she had a set limit she would drink and still drive home. This would be a good way around that if she didn't know how much she had to drink. She came back from the dance floor with a smile on her face.

"I ordered you another drink while you were gone."

"I usually don't have more than two drinks, but I guess one more won't hurt."

She finished the last of her other drink and sat down. "So, how come I have never seen you here before," she asked.

She took a sip of the new beer and looked at it like there was something off with it.

I said, "I think it is the bottom of the keg. It seems a little flat. But beer is beer, right?"

Then I said, "I'm just passing through, taking a few days to unwind and clear my head. So I decided to take a drive up the coast, and got a hotel a few blocks away for tonight."

"That's good information to know," she said, as she gave me a flirtatious smile.

I smiled back and said, "Let me buy you another beer."

"I can't have any more beer and drive. I already feel more buzzed than usual, but you can take me back to your hotel."

"That sounds like a great idea. Let me use the restroom and I will be right back to get you."

I stood up from the bar stool and walked to the back of the bar where the bathroom was located. Next to the bathroom was the back door. I never had any intention of taking her anywhere, but I did want her to look drunk and pissed off on her security camera when she got home.

I didn't get to see how she reacted when she found out I never paid for any drinks. While she was on the dance floor, I let the bartender know the nice lady said she would pick up the tap for me tonight. I imagine she sat there for a while before she realized I was not coming back. Hopefully, during this time she would finish her whole vodka beer. Then she probably got up to leave when the bartender stopped her to ask her to pay for all the drinks. If that didn't piss her off nothing would.

While all that was going on I was in a hurry to beat her back to her house. Only the front yard had security cameras, so I had to park two streets behind their house and jump some fences. I could not use the house directly behind Isabela's because it also had security cameras in the front yard. I had to go three houses down to the left to get a front yard I could walk across without a camera. Then I could hop all the backyard fences to get to Isabela's.

It was a hot night so I was hoping that the back-sliding glass door would be wide open with just the screen closed. It was. Isabela was in the kitchen. I put some boot covers over my shoes, and I already had my gloves on. I waited until she left the kitchen so I could sneak in and close the main glass door before she saw me.

I was sure she would scream. I needed that muffled as much as possible from the neighbors. I opened the screen door as slowly and quietly as possible. I walked through the screen but left it open. Then I closed the glass door as quietly as I could. I walked into the living room. I needed to get as close as I could to her as fast as possible in case she tried to run. Her back was to me, so I waited until I got just a foot away before I said to her, "Don't scream!"

She took a startled jump and turned around really quickly, but to my surprise, she did not scream. She just looked at me and said, "Why am I still alive?"

"What do you mean?" I asked.

"I knew this was coming but I just figured it would be over and I wouldn't know it even happened. What is the purpose of talking to me and scaring me before I die?"

This threw me off for a minute, but I had to get back to the job. "Enough talking. I know you have a gun in the house where, is it?" I asked.

"Now I see. They want you to make it look like a suicide. For a second, I thought that prick of a boss of mine was going to have you torture me. I will get you the gun, but I won't do it. I will not shoot myself. I'm a good person and am saved. I know I am going to be with the Lord, but I am in no way going to jeopardize any part of that by killing myself. You are going to be the one to kill me I will not help at all with that."

"You will do what I say, or your sister will be after you."

She smiled and said, "That's not a threat. To be honest I was hoping she would be home when you all came for me. She is a worthless piece of shit. I have taken care of her our whole life. She will just self-destruct when I am gone. That is one of the reasons I am still here. I told her we needed to leave. Just pick up and go. I told her I was in trouble, but she would not come with me. I should have just left her, but I made a promise to my mom that I would always look after her. I knew it would eat at me the rest of my life if I left her, and what life am I going to have any way out there with no money or job. No, going to be with God sounds better, but you would be doing her a favor killing her too. I don't know how she is going to live with no job or no money. There is no way she is going to get a job, but I guess after tonight that will no longer be my burden. After you do your job my promise to my mom will be fulfilled."

Isabel was telling me this on the way upstairs to her bedroom. "The gun is in the nightstand."

I walked over to the nightstand and took out the gun. I checked to make sure it was loaded which it was. Then I said, "Okay let's go back downstairs."

She looked puzzled again and asked, "What are you waiting for?"

I said, "Just go downstairs." While we were walking downstairs curiosity got the best of me. So, I asked her, "Why her company would want her dead?"

Isabel said she found out the new product they are selling does nothing. It doesn't hurt anyone, but it also does not help anyone. "I should have just left it alone, but I couldn't. If I could get someone from the FDA to work with me, I could prove it, but I didn't claim the drug was harmful, so they put me low on the priority list and they're just looking into it themselves. The partners have offered to pay me to let it go but I cannot. Without me helping the FDA it will take them years to realize the drug does not do what it is supposed to, but by then they will have made millions off the drug."

"So, you are willing to die over nothing. I got to be honest with you. You say you don't want any part of killing yourself, but it seems like this whole thing could have been easily avoided. To me, this almost feels like you are planning your suicide. Just because you are not pulling the trigger it still seems like you want it to happen."

"I just hope God does not see it that way."

Then she looked at me and said, "To be honest, I thought I was just being paranoid. I knew some of the partners were money-hungry, but I am close to one of them we used to talk all the time. I was nervous about it, but I guess I didn't think they would actually do it."

This was the first time I saw emotion on her face. She started to tear up as she said. "Again, what is with all the waiting? Why don't you just get it over with?"

Her comment about talking to one of the partners put all the pieces together for me, and with everything, she has told me I felt it would be okay to let her know the plan.

"Well Isabel, you're going to get your wish. We are going to wait for your sister to get home."

At that, she jumped up and came at me a little. I had to yell at her, "Sit back down!!"

She did as she started crying. "I did not mean it," she said.

"They have no reason to kill her she knows nothing. Please I do not want to be responsible for her death," she cried out.

I had to yell at her again, "Calm down! You are getting your wish. I am being paid to make it look like your sister killed you. Even in your death, you will be providing a roof over her head and three meals a day because she will be in prison the rest of her life."

This did calm her down. "The partner you talked to all the time must have come up with this plan to get you what you would want in a twisted sort of way."

I could tell Isabel was now processing a lot of emotions. The expressions on her face were changing every second. The last one was now turning to rage again before she said. "I do not have to sit here and make this easy for you."

I responded with, "You're right. You can try and fight me, but the outcome will be the same. You will die. The question is, what will happen to your sister? I can easily make this a murder-suicide instead of just a murder. That is your choice."

Just after I said that, a car pulled up the driveway and Isabel's sister got out. She shut the door to the car and started walking into the house. I looked at Isabel and said, "Be quiet," as I positioned myself behind the door. Her sister came in very abruptly slamming the front door. She walked in holding a bottle of vodka that was only one-quarter full. I had Chip put this in her front seat knowing she would carry this in the house in front of the security camera. After taking a few steps in she stopped and looked at her sister and said snidely. "What are you still doing up?"

Isabel just looked at her and said, "Why didn't you listen to me? I begged you to run away with me and we would be safe."

After she said this Isabel looked at me. Her sister turned around and saw me. She looked very confused. It was like she didn't even register that I was pointing a gun at her. She looked at me and said "What are you doing here? Are you here to pay me for the bar tab you stuck me with?"

I said, "Stay calm you don't have to get hurt."

She now noticed my gun and the fear started to sink in. She turned back to her sister as she put all the pieces together and said, "Am I really going to die here tonight because of you. You selfish bitch. I thought you were just paranoid. If you knew this was going to happen, why didn't you just leave? He wouldn't be here if you were not here."

Isabel said, "What would you do if I left without you. How would you afford anything and take care of yourself? I do everything for you. Me leaving you alone would be just the same as letting him kill you it would just take longer."

"I don't need you I can live on my own," her sister yelled.

"Then why haven't you," Isabel said.

"You have always thought you were better than me. Mom always thought you were better than me. Well, you're not. We are in this situation because of you. we are going to die because of you." Her sister said.

Isabel looked disgusted and said, "What does it make you happy to know I screwed up?"

Her sister then turned to me and said, "I do not need to be here. I promise I will not tell them I saw you. You can do what you want to her I promise I will never tell."

Isabela then said "You selfish bitch. You have never cared about anyone but yourself."

Her sister turned to Isabel to say more but I interrupted. "Okay enough! This has gone on long enough," I said.

Isabel then spoke up and said, "She may be a bitch, but you are not going to get her to shoot me."

I said, "Shut up." Then I positioned myself where I could have a gun on both of them. "This is what is going to happen."

I pulled a pill out of my top pocket and put it in Isabel's sister's hand. "Take that right now with the rest of that bottle of vodka."

She stared at me with scared eyes but did not move so I had to get more aggressive. I put the gun right on her forehead and said, "Take it now or die now."

She took the pill and finished the bottle. With the drinks from earlier that should put her tox screen high.

"This is what is going to happen. That pill will make sure you do not remember most of tonight. You may remember parts of driving home but everything from twenty minutes ago until now you will forget. You will not have to live with the image of your sister dying. You will be asleep in fifteen minutes and when you wake up your sister will be dead, and you will be holding the gun that killed her. Unfortunately, you will spend the rest of your life in prison but at least you will be alive."

She took her eyes off me and looked at Isabela and said, "You've ruined my life."

Isabel said, "Well if it wasn't for me you would never have had a life in the first place, so I guess we are even now."

Her sister then turned to me and said, "I will do it."

"Do what?" I said.

"I will kill her. Give me the gun. If I am going to prison for something, I want it to be something I did."

In all the different scenarios we planned for, this was not one. It did solve a lot of the cleanup and staging I would have to do. Now the gunpowder residue would be on her hand. I wouldn't have to fire another shot from the gun out of her hand and risk the neighbors hearing two separate shots. I was completely shocked, but I said, "Okay. But if you try anything other than shoot your sister you will die."

I moved behind her and said "I will hand this gun forward, but I am keeping my other gun on your head. Any other movements you will die."

After hearing how loud she slammed the door when she came in. I was betting this was a normal occurrence for these two women and the neighbors were used to it. I thought I would give myself some more time to get out of there and try and make sure it was me and Chip that called the police not one of the neighbors. I opened the front door. I handed her the gun and said, "On the count of three I will slam the door and you will shoot your sister."

Isabel looked at her holding the gun and said, "I can't believe you hate me this much. After all, I have done for you. You will go to hell for this."

I started to count. "One, two."

Isabel's sister said, "The only thing I will regret is that I don't get to remember this."

"Three," I said. Then I SLAMMED THE DOOR... She pulled the trigger and hit Isabel in the chest. She was only three feet from her so she could not miss. I ran to take the gun away from her.

"I can't believe I did it," she said. You're sure I won't remember?" she asked.

I sat her on the couch and said, "I am sure." She never took her eyes off her sister as she was bleeding out on the floor. I could tell the drug was starting to take effect making her sleepy. I sat with her for another five minutes until she was completely asleep. She tried fighting it and kept asking me if she would remember.

Then I went upstairs to grab the dresser drawer the gun was in. It probably didn't have her fingerprints on it, and I didn't want to leave anything for a jury to think about. I put her fingerprints on the knob of the drawer. Then I put the drawer back. Then I headed out the back door the same route I came in. Chip picked me up on the street. We gave it about three hours for the drug to start to wear off before we drove by the front of the house. We picked a car with deeply tented windows so the camera wouldn't pick us up.

Chip called 911 and told them as I was driving by a house, I thought I saw and heard a gunshot. He gave them the address and hung up. We swapped the car out with a different car. Waited about thirty minutes then drove back by the house to watch the cops pulling a very confused girl out of the house in hand cuffs. The rest was up to the cops. We flew back home that night and Chip accepted the money for the job. Now we just had to wait for the next one.

Chapter Six
First Mission 1.2

We didn't have to wait long after we got back home to get the next mission. The next day we got a new hit on the board. It was John John. This seemed a little odd to me, but Chip accepted the job and closed it right away. When we got the instructions, we found out it was not a real job, but it was NOA. It looked like we finally got his attention. The instructions said, "I am not sure how you found out about this board, but it's not open to the public. Stay off it or there will be consequences."

I had Chip reply with a price tag of 1 billion dollars and instructions that said pay me 1 billion and I will be gone. Otherwise, I like it here and will stay. I am better than you and will keep collecting as many checks as I can. You have no way to stop me.

NOA rejected the payment option. Chip tried to track down his servers but like all the times before they were gone by the time Chip found them.

The next day another job was posted to the board with the name John Jill. Chip open and closed the job. The instructions came back for a woman named Jill and an exact place and time to kill her. It instructed us that she goes for a run every morning and they wanted her shot on that run in two days. Chip sent the payment instruction for $450,000 USD to accept the job. This was rejected and a reoffer of $100,000 USD was sent back with the explanation that all the details were set, and they would turn somewhere else if we did not want the job for that price.

While the back-and-forth emails were going on we looked up the target and something didn't add up. This was just a single mom on welfare with two kids. From her Facebook page, it didn't look like she had many friends and no family. I told Chip to deny the request. I was not going to be part of orphaning two kids. Then Chip made a point that denying the request was the same as killing her. Someone else would just take on the job. This led us to the discussion of the lowball price being a setup by NOA. In the last email, NOA said there would be consequences for us accepting more jobs.

We could deny the request and let him take it. We knew the time and place but if this was a setup by NOA and we rejected the job there would be no reason for NOA to go there at all. We had to take the job and hope NOA would show up. This could be our opportunity to catch NOA.

Chip accepted the job, and we flew out within the hour. I started using Goggle earth to plan the shooting lanes and the obvious places to shoot from. This would be either on the roof or from the top window of the house at the end of the street. Management flew with us this time and other agents were also flying in to help catch NOA if NOA tried to take me out. We would need more than just me and Chip to track down the location and capture NOA.

It took a lot of convincing from me, but I finally talked management out of killing Jill. They didn't want to take the chance of letting NOA know that we are an organization and not just a rival assassin. I had to stand my ground firmly letting them know I would not pull the trigger. They said if I could come up with a full-proof plan that made it look like we killed her then we could move forward.

We only had a day to get all the moving parts in action. I planned to get a female agent that looked as close as we could to Jill. She would do Jill's morning run for her. We would hide exploding red dye packs as they use in the movies on the front and back of her head. This would have to match for an angle from a shooter from the house at the end of the street. I would then place a dummy with a rifle in one of the windows at the end of the street. There would still need to be an agent in the room with the dummy. The agent would need to move the dummy while staying out of the way of the window. If NOA never saw the dummy moving it may raise suspicion and NOA may never shoot. The ideal solution would be to have a live person in the window, but that would basically be asking someone to commit suicide if this was a setup. We would only raise the dummy a few seconds before the shot and start to move it away right after the shot. This is how a real assassin would work. NOA would have to shoot quickly and not have much time in a real situation.

For the second part of the plan, we would need to find a freshly dead female body from the morgue. She would have to be the same height and build as Jill. We would need to put a bullet through her head so this would have to be someone with no family, but I was going to leave that up to the agency to handle.

While I was glad, we were saving Jill's life. She and her kids were still going to be victims and their lives were going to change forever. The best scenario would be that we catch NOA. Then at least we would know NOA planned the hit, but even with that Jill and her family would still have to go into protective services. They would need a new identity and would be living new lives.

If we don't catch NOA, then we will have to make it look like Jill died and the kids will have to go into foster care for at least a few months. After that time, we would have Jill adopt her kids back under a new alias but either way, they will have to start living new lives.

We arrived late that night and started to prepare. We took a few drives up the street and surveillance the situation. We only had one day to learn the habits of all the neighbors and try and finalize the plan. While doing our surveillance we found a house that was a few houses up from Jill's that had three newspapers stacked up in the driveway. We looked up the credit cards of the owners of the house and found some charges from New Orleans on it. It looks like they are on vacation. We looked up their flight information and they were not coming home for another three days. It was still late, so Chip and I broke into the house from the back and decided to use that house to do all the surveillance for the next day. We were also going to post an agent in the house on the day of the shooting to watch for NOA. This would be the perfect house to shoot our assassin from and it may not be a coincidence that it has no one in it.

The next day we got up early and started watching all the people in the neighborhood. We did this from small camera wires we put out the windows. We were sure some of the neighbors would know the people that lived in this house were on vacation so we could not be seen in the house looking out the windows. It was a Tuesday we felt safe to assume that everyone's routine would be the same today as it would be tomorrow, but I still wanted to plan for everything.

The events we wanted to look for, were multiple cars leaving for the day. That would suggest the house is empty and available for us to enter. The house we picked from Google Earth did not work out for us. That house had a stay-at-home mom in it. However, the one to the right of it had both cars leave before 8:00 am. Jill's run was at 9:00 a.m. every morning so that gave us a full hour to prepare. It was going to give NOA a harder shot to kill the dummy depending on where NOA chose to set up for the shot. The best place would be the house we were in but that is so obvious if I was trying to outwit another assassin, I do not think I would pick it for that reason. The house three houses up the street from Jill also had both cars go to work. This could be used as our second option if both cars did not leave on time from the house at the end of the street. It would not be ideal because if NOA was set up for the shot on that side of the street the shot would not be possible to make. Then we would have to catch NOA leaving the house.

The whole time I was coming up with my plan I was also trying to plan how I would shoot me if I was NOA. If I could come up with all options on both sides, then it should be easier to capture NOA. The only problem with that is if I miss one option and get outsmarted then I put my life and the life of my agents in jeopardy.

We spent the rest of the day tracking all the activity of the neighborhood. Taking notes and going over every outcome and scenario we could think of. The final plan did not change much from the original plan we came up with on the plane. One of the changes was put in place because of Jill's neighbor. During Jill's morning run, she waved, "hi" to her as she was sitting on her porch drinking coffee. This was about the same spot we wanted to make the fake shot on Jill. We had to be the first people to get to our down agent. Up close you would be able to tell the wound was not real. So now we were going to time a car driving up the street toward Jill. The driver would be the one to get out of the car and run to Jill immediately. They would tell the neighbor to go inside and call 911 and our standby ambulance would be there before she came back out. If she was not on the porch then we would not have the real 911 call, we would just have the ambulance show up. The response time for both scenarios would be way quicker than normal, but that just means the backend work will have to be convincing if we do not catch NOA during the shooting.

With all the planning completed, I decided to get a few hours of sleep. My mind was tired from all the over-planning, and I wanted to be fresh for tomorrow. My part in all the action would be minimal the next day. No one in our agency knew me and Chip existed, and management wanted to keep it that way. They were going to run the plan and act like they came up with it. Chip and I were only to show ourselves if we were in pursuit of NOA. Other than that, I was going to be a spotter with a rifle watching all the directions the shooter would take out our assassin from. If I found NOA setup before the shot, I would call it in, and the team would take NOA alive. If I found him after the shot, I would try and shoot NOA so NOA could not escape. Chip was going to set off the blood packs on the agent's face and also try to spot NOA.

The next morning, we all got into our position. Two agents had to sneak into Jill's basement and hide out at 3:00 a.m. One was the agent that was doing Jill's run and the other was an agent to explain the situation to Jill. They also had to sneak Jill out the back at the same time the fake Jill went out the front for the run. The agents were going to stay hidden until after Jill took her kids to the bus. We didn't want the kids to know anything about the plan. They were going to have to act as if their mom was dead.

I was positioned in a backyard between a shed and a fence. It was one of the houses that would be empty after both the adults went to work. I also had to get there early in the morning so I could use the darkness not to be seen. I cut a large hole in the lower part of the fence to look through. It would be easy to spot me if my head was above the fence. I would have to watch from down low. It also gave me a good prone shooting position if I did find NOA first.

I kind of felt like the JFK shooter from the grassy knoll. That may have just been me joking with myself to try and calm myself down. I was more nervous this time than on the other missions. It may be because this was the mission. The other assignments were just to get to this point. We had a lot of time and effort into catching NOA, and it all could end today if I did my job right.

It was close to time now. Jill was walking back from dropping off her kids. She went into the house. This would be the time the agents would grab her. They would start explaining the situation to her and start moving her to the back of the house. I didn't have much time now. I was looking everywhere. I looked in every window and on every roof that I thought I would hide at. I was looking through my scope, and without my scope. Every spot I looked at was empty. Come on let me see something. Let me find someone. My heart was racing now as anger was starting to set in.

The fake agent Jill was now opening the door and starting the jog. She turned onto the sidewalk. I was going window to window looking for NOA. Now I started to second guess myself. What if NOA was behind me? I do not see anyone anywhere. NOA must be behind me. Should I look? The agent is still running if I look now, I will not see the shot.

I started to see the dummy being raised in the window. I must fight the urge to look at it. I must watch for the secondary shot. I tried but from the corner of my eye, I see the flash of the muzzle from the dummy gun. The agent goes down. The die packs go off. I still don't see anyone. The car slams on its breaks the agent gets out of the car and runs to the down agent. Still no shot. The dummy is back out of sight now.

The neighbor is on the porch. The agent yells at her to call 911. She wants to come out and see Jill. The agent must get aggressive with her to go call 911. I can't find anyone in any window or on any roof. The neighbor goes into the house and calls 911. I start to hear the sirens from our ambulance. I still can't see anybody anywhere. My heart drops. NOA is not here. Our only other chance is that NOA will try and strike when the agent with the dummy tries to leave the house. That was one of the other ideas I came up with. If I wanted to kill an assassin. Rather than trying to make the quick and tough shot when they make their shot. I would just try and kill them as they leave the house they just shot from. We have an agent setup to watch this, but I know it is a long shot. The ambulance is now pulling away. They will replace the agent with the dead body and now the kids will be in foster care.

The next few days are going to be hard on this family. I sit at my location for the next few hours to let all the commotion settle down. Then I meet Chip at the meeting point. "I guess we are flying back home empty-handed," I said to him.

"Yep, back to the drawing board," Chip said.

We arrived back at our base and Chip sent out the completion notice. We got the payment almost immediately. With it were some comments that said. Congratulations you just killed an innocent woman with two children. Now those children will have to grow up without a mom. I hope you can live with yourself. I just needed you out of the way, so you did not steal my next job. It will be a big one. Thanks again.

Chip checks the job board. Within the hour we were sent to kill Jill a job was opened with the name John Anton. That son of a bitch was not there to kill us. We were just played. I was angry, but I still had to laugh. I told Chip to reply with. I did not kill an innocent mom you did. You sent the order I just pulled the trigger and the hundred grand you gave me will help me sleep just fine. Thanks for giving me part of the cut of your next job. If you want in the future just send me one hundred grand from every job you do. Thanks again.

Hopefully, that would piss NOA off enough to keep wanting to engage with me. We now knew NOA was going to be off on another job so we would have some time to regroup. I wanted to accelerant the training. I did not feel as confident as I should have sitting by the shed on the last mission.

Chip and management had to go do some research to look for any important people named Anton. I also wanted Chip to see if we could find out a way to post jobs to the job board. It would be nice if we could give NOA a job with a set time and date.

Chapter Seven
First Mission 1.3

It had been over a month since we were on our last mission. Chip and management never found Anton. Management was not ready to try and post a mission to the job board. Our first failed attempt at accepting the job had probably already set up some red flags. NOA had already contacted us, and they liked that progress. They didn't want to risk alerting NOA that we were anything other than a rival assassin.

I had been working hard on my training. Getting into shape trying to learn as much as I could about different combat situations. While training one morning I heard Chip say we got another job. The job came in John Jacob. Chip closed out the job with the contract price in it. Normally the replies were within minutes but this time we waited over two hours before the response came back. When we got the response, it came back with a request denied. There was no counteroffer or reason why. This seemed odd. Chip started looking back at the board to see if the job would be reposted. We waited a few hours, but the job was never reposted.

I told Chip to go back to the job board to see if the job came in differently than all the other jobs. Chip went back and looked. It was just like all the other jobs. But while looking back Chip noticed that in-between the time, we accepted the job, and the rejection offer came in another job was posted and closed. NOA had gotten us again and this time it did not cost anything. This meant I would now have to start learning how to do some of Chip's jobs. I was going to have to watch the board every time Chip accepted new jobs.

The job we missed was interesting. The name was John Rajiv Pramod. We had never seen three names before. Could it be that they put their first and last name on the board? We could not find anyone named Rajiv Pramod, but the search did pop up two Indian investors that were on the verge of a building deal in New York. The names were too specific not to be them. It was still going to be hard to catch NOA because we did not have a time and date, but this was the first time we might be one step ahead of NOA. Just as we were planning out the trip to New York another job came in on the job board. It was John Jacob again. This proposed an interesting development. We could not accept a job and go chase NOA, but we also could not be a rival assassin and let a job go. I told Chip to more than double the cost. If this was NOA putting us on another wild goose chase, then let's make it hurt the pocketbook. The price was denied but a counteroffer did come back. It was NOA. In the instruction was an explanation that this was going to be the first of three double assassinations. NOA wanted us to work together. The instructions read that it would be obvious who the targets were and NOA did not want us interfering with the job. So NOA would plan the next three jobs telling us what to do and pay us more than the going rate we were getting. We just had to let NOA accept the next two job postings and after each one he would send his job to us under the name John Jacob. We would get paid if we followed the instructions. The instruction also said if we did this, we could have the job board all to ourselves. If all three jobs go well, I will be retiring.

Chip accepted the terms with the new payment.

I had a mix of emotions. On one hand, the first advantage we were ever going to have on NOA was gone. On the other hand, we knew for sure we will now be getting in close contact with NOA. The biggest problem was it would all be on NOA's terms. Now we will get to see who is smarter, I guess. I wasn't quite sure I believed NOA wanted to retire. The obvious option would be that NOA wanted to retire me. I hope I am ready for this.

The next day we got on a plane to New York. We were not going to get any help on this mission from the agency. The last mission with Jill put up a lot of suspicion for the owners from the other board member. They were asking a lot of questions about how they found out about Jill, so the bosses deemed it too risky to involve anyone but me and Chip for the rest of the missions.

We landed in New York and checked in to our hotel. Chip and I started doing all the research we could about Rajiv and Pramod. I wanted to have a head start on any plan NOA could come up with. I wanted to go start surveillance on them to see if I could find NOA tailing them, but we soon found out that would be harder than expected. Rajiv and Pramod were not in New York yet. They both were due to arrive on Wednesday. Their flights were landing within twenty minutes of each other. This must be why NOA needed help. Pramod would be out of the airport by the time Rajiv landed. This was going to be easier than I thought. All we would have to do is tail the one that NOA did not give us. Finally, we would be able to capture NOA.

Later that night we received the instructions. NOA wanted us to act as the limo driver and pick up Pramod. We were to have a selection of high-end cigars in the back seat waiting for him. NOA wanted us to inject all the cigars with Botox. Pramod received regular injections of Botox so it would be a chemical that would be explained in his tox screen. While Botox is not lethal when injected it is highly lethal when ingested. It is a neurotoxin that will mirror the same symptoms of a stroke. We were also instructed to dispose of all the cigars and drive him to the hospital after the reaction started. It would be too late for the hospital to save him.

We had two days to prepare. We had to acquire a limo, high-end cigars, and some Botox. Chip found a distributor of Botox in New York. He looked up the delivery route for the next day. I just waited for them to make their first delivery. While the driver was inside, I broke into the truck and took two vials. One from two different boxes. We only need one vial, but I thought it best to have a backup. It only takes 0.3 micrograms to be lethal.

Chip got the limo and the cigars. Now we were all set. I spent the next day at the JFK airport learning all the streets in and out. Familiarizing myself with the terminals. Especially the ones Rajiv and Pramod would be landing at. I was also careful to look like a traveler. NOA could be doing the same thing as me, so

I had to scout without scouting. Watch others without looking like I was watching others. It was a very stressful day. My mind was on high alert all day. I was second-guessing everything. Was I being too casual? Was I looking too hard at everyone? Was it obvious that I was checking out all the exits? Did I go into too many bathrooms? Has that guy been here all day like me, or did it just look like someone from earlier in the day? It takes a lot of energy to look calm when inside everything is going a hundred miles an hour, but this is what I had to learn to control.

I was glad Chip was not with me. After several hours I had gotten the information that I needed. Now I was going to go back to the hotel to start planning and over planning every option. Hopefully, tomorrow will be the day we finally catch NOA.

Back at the hotel Chip and I went over both our plans. Chip was going to be the driver for Pramod. It would be cutting it close but with only two of us I was going to have to do two jobs. I would watch the surrounding area to cover Chip. If this was a setup Chip was going to be a sitting duck. We found as much cover as we could for Chip. I wanted him standing with his back against a pillar to the outside. While holding the sign for Pramod. It would be unlikely that NOA would try and sneak a rifle into the airport. NOA would likely step outside for a shot. We found a path that would make it difficult to get a shot off. Well at least until they arrived at the car.

Chip was just going to have to hope that this job was on the up and up. The route we picked would also allow Chip to hide his face from most of the security cameras. We had to make this look like a professional job. That was another reason Chip would be the driver. If NOA set up his own camera or was watching us, we didn't want NOA seeing my face. If we didn't catch NOA today I still needed to be able to be undetected in the next two missions.

After Chip was in the car with Pramod I would then have to hurry. I needed to get to Rajiv's gate before his plane landed. I would watch him get off the plane and follow him. Hopefully all the way to NOA. It would be tricky when to engage NOA. I could not be sure NOA's plan was the same as ours. I could not assume the driver was NOA and if I engage the driver and it is not NOA then we would most likely lose NOA forever.

I didn't sleep much that night I kept running different scenarios on how to engage NOA the next day. I think NOA would be too smart to show up as the driver. My best option would be to tail the car and try and watch for Rajiv to fall over, but I felt like if I let the car leave the parking lot without engaging NOA that my chances of failing increase tremendously. I also had to remember that if Chip does his job well and this is not a setup that I will have two other chances to catch NOA. It was like I was the quarterback. It's first and ten with one minute on the clock. If the play is not there, then I need to throw the ball away rather than risk an interception.

I ate breakfast at the hotel then caught a cab to the airport. I had one duffel bag and one travel bag. The duffel bag had my rifle in it. It would stay outside the airport to cover Chip if needed. The travel bag was just so I would blend in with the rest of the travelers while I was inside the airport. I had a good spot behind a trash can to hide my duffel bag. It would be easy to place once Chip left and easy to grab leaving the airport if I wanted to pursue NOA. It was also in a location I felt would be okay if I had to leave it overnight.

I wanted to get to the airport a few hours early and start watching for other suspicious people, but I was more worried that I would stand out. Not too many people stand in front of an airport for hours, so I shortened my time so I would only be there twenty minutes before Chip.

First, I went and hid the duffel bag behind the trash can. Then I bought a paper and sat outside to read it on the bench by my rifle. This was a position out of the camera view. Chip was right on time. It was hard to holdup the large paper and see everything else that was going on. So, I put down the paper and picked up my phone. Chip went and stood on his pillar waiting for Pramod. There were a lot of people walking around. I kept fake playing on my phone, but I could not see anything out of the ordinary.

Pramod came out right on time. Chip did a good job of standing his ground and making Pramod come all the way to him at the pillar. Chip took his bag from him and walked him to the car. I started to feel like I was not in a good position. I would not be able to see a shooter from far off. I had to fight off the urge to go for the gun. I did not see any reason to have it, but I sure would feel better with it.

Chip made it to the car and used the remote to open the trunk. This should give him a little more cover. Chip opened the door and sat Pramod inside the car using the car door for cover. Chip put Pramod's bag in the trunk and walked around to get in the driver's seat.

I felt helpless again but that all went away fast. Chip was in the car and started driving away. I had anxiety and disappointment all over again. I needed to hurry and get to Rajiv gate, but I wanted to wait a few minutes. It would be obvious if I left right after Chip left to anyone watching from far. I sat there for four minutes then got up and went inside.

The security line was longer than expected. I made sure I could use the priority line, but this was still going to be closer than I would like. I had fifteen minutes now until Rajiv's plane landed. I made it through security and to the gate. The plane had landed but people were not yet walking off the plane. There was an open seat at the gate right next to the agent's desk. My ticket was for the next flight on that plane. It may have been an over kill but better to be prepared for anything. People were coming off the plane now. Rajiv was first class so I would expect him to be one of the first off. I continued watching but I didn't see him. Over half the plane was off now and still no Rajiv. I continued watching, almost everyone was off now, and I still did not see him.

By now there were no more people coming off the plane. I asked the stewardess if there were more people on the plane, she said, "No."

How could I have missed him? I know what Rajiv looks like. I could not have missed him. There was nothing else I could do. Now I had to try and catch up to all the rest of the passengers. I didn't want to run but I had to be brisk. My over-planning may have cost me this time. The drivers could not come to the gate I should have just stayed out with the drivers and caught him there. I recognized some of the other passengers on the plane and started to follow them out the airport.

I saw some customers now over by the luggage claim. I could still not see him. I continued to follow the passengers out toward the drivers and suddenly out of the corner of my eye, I saw a sign with Rajiv's name on it.

Keep walking. Don't stare. Was this NOA? I kept walking closer. I walked right past him getting a good look at the driver holding the sign. I walked past far enough but not all the way to the doors. I turned around and his back was still to me. I went and found a seat in the corner to watch.

The luggage was now coming off the plane. I watched most of the passengers as they got their luggage and left the airport. The driver was still standing there holding the sign for Rajiv. I pulled out my phone again to act like I was looking at it. While it was out, I started snapping a few photos of the driver. All the passengers from the plane were now gone and you could tell the driver was confused. This could not be NOA. Something went very wrong with the plan. The driver started to walk up to the counter. I wanted to follow him, but I would never make it in time.

There was no way I could engage this driver. I went outside and found the limo with no driver in it. I placed a tracking device in the wheel well. Then went back to the airport. The driver was still talking to the desk agent. I stayed back and watched until the driver got back in the limo and drove away.

I knew what the driver must have asked the agent, but I did not want to go to the same one. That would be too obvious to anyone watching. So, I went to a different desk and asked a different agent the same question I assumed the driver did.

"Hi, ma'am, I am here to pick up a passenger that should have been on flight UA 522 can you please tell me if they were on the flight." I gave the agent Rajiv's name.

"I am sorry to inform you, sir. That passenger never made the flight. It seems the customer had a heart attack while waiting for the flight in the San Francisco airport."

I immediately turned and walked away. I heard her in the background saying, "I am extremely sorry for your loss."

NOA wasn't even in New York. Rajiv had a layover in San Francisco and that is where NOA got him. Walking out of the airport I took a good hard look at the bar. It wasn't like I was going to be needed tonight. I stood in front of it for a few minutes and thought hard about it, but after a few minutes I calmed down. I still have two more opportunities at this. I also needed to get back to the hotel to regroup with Chip. I still wasn't sure how his mission went. It should be done by now if everything went okay.

I got back to the hotel before Chip. I decided to see where the limo was that I put the tracker on. It looks like it was back at the same rental place Chip rented our limo from. Something didn't seem right about that situation, but I could not put my finger on it. I started looking at all the pictures I took of the limo driver. One of them caught his back just right. I can't believe I did not notice it in person. The driver was carrying a gun. Why would a limo driver need a gun? This was not sitting well with me. If NOA had an accomplice, then why didn't NOA just not use that person to kill Pramod? Unless that driver was a patsy to see if we would engage him? That still didn't make any sense. If NOA had any help the job was so easy there would be no reason to engage us. No NOA did not know that driver. That still leaves the question of who sent that driver?

Just about then Chip showed back up. Everything went as planned. I had Chip call the hospital to ask about the condition of Pramod and they confirmed he was dead. Then I told Chip lets destroy the remaining cigars. Then we can send the e-mail for the payment. When I said that, Chip asked, "What do you mean destroy the cigars? I already threw them away."

"Threw them away where Chip?" I asked.

"In a trash can just outside the hospital. That was the plan, right?"

"No Chip the plan was to destroy them. What if some bum digs through that trash can, then goes and hands out a bunch of cigars to his bum friends and all of them end up dead with the same symptoms as Pramod? Go back and get them now." It was lucky that the cigars were still there when Chip went back to get them.

After Chip got back, we burned all the cigars in a trash can fire. Making sure we were far enough away not to inhale any of the smoke. Chip also sent the final payment order, and we were paid. I started to review all my concerns with Chip about Rajiv's driver. Chip did not share my concerns. "A lot of drivers rent limos for one-time jobs," Chip said.

We reviewed the whole job with management. I told them I was going to go down to the limo rental to see what I could find out about the driver. They also told me it was a waste of time and wanted me to start working on the next mission. They said they would follow up on it. Something still did not seem right to me, but I decided to let it go.

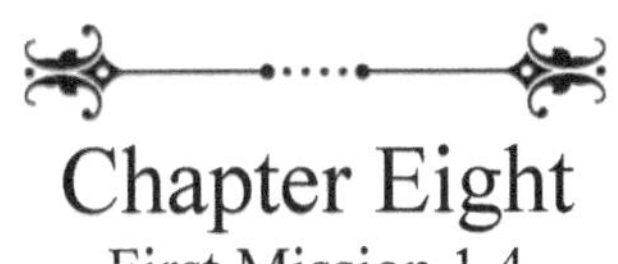

Chapter Eight
First Mission 1.4

We decided not to fly back to the training facility this time. We rented a VRBO for the next few weeks. We were hoping it would not take long for the next job to come in, and we didn't want to be in transition if it came in right away. There were a lot of discussions if we should try and steal the job. I wanted to so we could determine how the job would unfold, but management said it was not worth the risk of scaring off NOA especially if this would be our last chance before NOA retires.

It was a long week sitting around the house waiting for the next job to come in. I was not good at sitting around doing nothing. The last six months of my life had me constantly thinking about a mission or training. My mind had not been idle like this for a long time, and it was driving me crazy. I was going for long runs, three to four times a day, but even running was not helping the anxiety that an idle mind was giving me. I also couldn't get the last mission off my mind. Maybe it was because that was the only thing I had to think about, but something about that driver was just not right.

I got back from one of my runs. As I came through the door Chip said, "It's in. The job came in."

The name on the job was John Peter Ivan. Chip left the job alone and it didn't take NOA long to grab it and close it. We got started right away researching people with the first names Peter and Ivan, but nothing obvious was standing out. The names were just too common. We spent the next four hours working on it but the more time that went by the less concentration I had. I keep thinking what if NOA had gotten over on us again. The plan for the last job was in two different cities. This one may be easy for one person to handle. NOA could have just put us off accepting the last few jobs. NOA could complete this job and disappear forever. There could be no third job.

It had been one full week since the job came in and we still had not received instruction or a listing for a job to help NOA. My metal capacity was not in very good shape. I was only getting three to four hours of sleep a night. My runs were getting longer and longer. I couldn't stand being idle anymore.

I was still asking management to let me spend my time looking into the driver for Rajiv's car or to send me to San Francisco to try and look at security tapes at the airport. If we followed Rajiv through the airport, we should be able to get an image of NOA. They kept telling me they had people looking at all that and I just needed to be ready for when the next job came in. I asked them what if the next job never comes in. We are just wasting time then.

I made it another two days then I couldn't take it anymore. I needed to sleep, and I knew the only way that was going to happen was to get a few drinks in me. I had been sober for six months but I didn't care anymore. I didn't want to spend another night looking at the ceiling. There was a local bar down the street. I told Chip I was going down there to get dinner that I was tired of takeout. Chip just said, "Okay."

I could tell there was going to be no offer from him to go with me. We were starting to get on each other's nerves, and I could tell Chip was relieved to have the place to himself for the night.

When I got there, I decided to just sit at the bar. I started with a beer and some food. After I finished all the food, I had another beer and a shot of Jager. I don't remember much after the first five beers. I didn't talk to anybody I just remember watching the football game that was on and drinking beer after beer.

I don't think I closed the place down that night, and I did manage to get back to the VRBO just fine. I woke up the next morning and to my surprise, it was already 8:00 am. My plan had worked. Finally, I slept through the night. My body didn't feel like I had gotten a full night's sleep. I was still tired, and I had a headache that would not go away, but my mind seemed to be rested.

My mind finally had a chance to wind down. I didn't spend all night thinking about all the things I could not control, and that was worth the headache and tiredness. I went into the kitchen to get a cup of coffee then went and sat on the back deck. I sat there for almost an hour before my anxiety started coming back. My body didn't feel like a run but at this point, I had no other mechanism to cope with the anxiety. I put on my running gear and went out for a jog. My pace was slower than normal. I didn't have the drive today. I ran to my halfway point and decided that was enough. I turned around and ran back to the VRBO.

When I walked through the door Chip said, "That was way shorter than normal." I didn't even reply to him. I just went back to my room to lay on the bed. I ended up falling back asleep. I woke up about two hours later and I was feeling pretty good. I went out and Chip had lunch delivered. I ate lunch and asked Chip if there was anything we could do but we had already exhausted all the research we could do. I sat around going stir crazy again for the next four hours. Then I finally gave up." I am going back out to the bar to eat dinner again" I told Chip.

The next four days and nights played out the same as the first one did except for the amount of alcohol I was consuming was increasing each time. One night I was getting tired of setting at the bar by myself and started talking to another regular that had been there every night with me. She wasn't the prettiest thing I had ever seen but she was by no means ugly either. She had tried to talk to me a few times before, but I never responded. To my surprise, she didn't make any mention of that when I started up a conversation with her. She was just willing to move over to talk and drink with me all night. I did close the bar that night.

Then the next night started just like we never left the bar. I paid for her dinner and a few drinks. We were about four hours into the night when she asked me if I wanted to get out of there and go back to her place. I didn't even hesitate. I was ready. "Let's go," I said.

I paid my tab, and we started walking out. Before we made it out the door Chip walked in and grabbed me and said, "We need to go. The job came in."

"Are we going to do the job tonight?"

"No, but you need to be rested let's go."

"I'll be back in the morning. I will be good to go tomorrow. Just let me have tonight."

Chip grabbed my arm and said "What are you doing? Are you going to let everything we worked for go away for a one-night stand? We have a chance to get NOA. Let's go get him."

I was really drunk but, at that moment, I realized Chip was right. I said, "Sorry" to my new lady friend, and I left with Chip.

When we got back home, I wanted to start working on the plan, but chip would not discuss anything with me. "You're drunk. Go to bed. We will start work tomorrow when you sober up."

I wasn't too happy but still drunk enough not to care. I went to bed as Chip asked.

The next morning, I didn't sleep in like the four days before. I was up at 5:00 am. I ate breakfast and went for a short morning run to try and clear my head of the cobwebs of a five-day bender. When I got back, I was surprised to see that Chip was already awake. I was going to wake him up but now I didn't have to.

Chip started right away going over the job with me. It seems about one hour after I left last night the John Jacob job came in. Chip accepted it and closed it like all the times before. It took about three more hours before the instructions came in. When they came in is when Chip went to go get me from the bar. "We should have started this last night," Chip said.

"Get over it. What's done is done let's move on with it."

The job was going to be in three days. Iven and Peter were going to meet a real estate agent onsite to buy an old building in New York. This was the same building Rajiv and Pramod were in town to buy.

Iven and Peter were part of the Russian mob. What would two Indian investors and the Russian mob want with the same building? I told Chip to look up who else were potential buyers for the building.

"Let's get to that later. We only have three days to get everything set up," Chip said.

Most of the other buildings around the one for sale were also vacant. NOA wants us to set up on the fourth floor in the first room on the right side of the building. I told Chip to let NOA know we would set up where we wanted to. No assassin would set themselves up that easy. NOA agreed that we could setup wherever we wanted but wanted to let us know that would make for the easiest shot.

I had Chip ask NOA where they would be shooting from, but same as me NOA did not reply with that information. The plan was to shoot Ivan and Peter as soon as they shook hands. If they did not shake hands when they met. Then we were to shoot them exactly one minute after the last one got out of their car. NOA provided pictures of Ivan and Peter. I was to shoot Peter. NOA would shoot Ivan.

We started doing our research on Ivan and Peter and they were some real scum bags. They did everything from human trafficking to drugs. They had never been in the real-estate market and were not even from New York. They were from Miami. They would be flying in for this meeting just like Rajiv and Pramod did. It didn't make sense why we weren't taking them out the same way. We could have done the same plan as we did for Rajiv and Pramod.

This job was not made to look like an accident. This one was made to look like a rival gang hit them. Even still we could have shot them in the limo and still had the same effect.

NOA warned us not to go to the site and prepare for this hit. NOA said if anyone was spotted scouting the area the mission would be called off. The instructions were to just show up one hour before Iven and Peter would be there. Make the shot and get out. That is the only way we would get paid.

I wanted to ignore this, but management stepped in again letting us know we had to make all the plans from Google maps. They did not want to take the chance of blowing this job and not being able to catch NOA.

We downloaded the design plans for all the surrounding buildings. NOA was right the best shot would be from the fourth floor in the last office. It was high enough the cars could not block you and it would be a straight shot to the front of the building where they would park. The two offices below would work too. It would just be easier to see the muzzle flash for people standing on the ground level. We knew Ivan and Peter will have armed guards with them, so our plan needs to include a way to get out of there without getting shot by their men.

Normally management stayed out of the planning. Chip and I always reviewed the final plan with them, but this time they were right in the middle of it looking over our shoulders. We just called them Number One, Two, and Three. It was cheesy but I did like it better than some acronym about me.

Number One and Three were on board with me. I wanted to make our plan to catch NOA and killing Peter would be an afterthought if that failed. Number

Two was the complete opposite. Number Two was adamant that there would still be one more mission to catch NOA if this one failed but there would be no next mission if we did not kill Peter. Number Two was so adamant that eventually, the other two chairmen submitted to his request.

This changed the planning dramatically. Now the first plan was how to set up to kill Peter and the second plan was how to shoot or capture NOA once we learned the position NOA was at. NOA asked us to shoot from the building across the streets so I didn't think NOA would be in the same building with us. NOA was too smart for that. If NOA was not in the building with us that would only leave the parking garage to the right of the building. That way NOA would be able to see my shot and have a possible shot back at me if that would be the intent. Number Two was still adamant that there was another mission so NOA would not try and kill me on this one. The one thing we did know was that NOA would not be in the building that was for sale. That would be a straight down shot and you would have to hang out a window to make the shot. It would also be the place Peter and Ivan's men would run for cover. So, no assassin would put themselves in a situation to have to escape a building with people that wanted to kill you. It would however be a good place to set up to watch all the action. You would be able to see any shot from the parking garage or the building across the street.

So, the decision was to put Chip there. Chip would also have a rifle and could shoot any shooters in the parking garage. I would be in the building across the street. If NOA was in that building after I shot Peter,

Chip would be able to tell me what floor and room the shot came from, and I could go to try and capture NOA. I voiced my opinion several times that NOA would not be in that building or the parking garage. NOA has always put a twist on every mission and this one would be no different. While they agree they said we could not come up with a better plan. If we did not catch NOA then we would still have one more mission and they promised in the next one, we would not worry at all about the target just about catching NOA.

The final plan ended up with me being one room over from the room NOA suggested. They said NOA thought it was the best place to shoot from and now NOA knew we would not be in that room. Maybe the twist would be NOA would choose that room to take the shot. If that happen after I shot Peter, I could just go next door and shoot NOA. I just rolled my eyes and let it go after they said the plan was final. We still had two days left until Ivan and Peter came in, so management asks us to take it easy and rest tomorrow. They did not want us to leave the house and gave us strict instructions not to visit the site. I told them I still planned one very long run in the morning but that I would take the afternoon off. They ended up leaving around 11:00 pm and Chip and I went to bed.

The next morning, I tried to sleep in, but the best I could do was 7:00 am. I decided to take my time and eat a good breakfast before my morning run. Chip made a comment coming out of his room at 8:00 am. "I didn't expect to see you here. Why aren't you running?"

I let him know that I would be leaving soon. Not to worry and not to expect me back anytime soon. I was going to push myself today for my longest run yet. I left about 30 minutes later around 8:30 am, and I did push myself hard. I had a lot to think about and I still wanted to go over every scenario I could think of in my mind. This mission was giving me a bad feeling in my stomach. There was something that did not feel right so I wanted to be prepared for any situation I could think of.

I got back about five hours after I left. When I walked through the door Chip looked at me and said, "Man, you had me nervous. I know you said you would be long, but five hours is long."

I said, "Sorry I had a lot to think about."

Then I asked him to sit down. "Chip," I said. "Something does not feel right with this mission, and I am going to change it. I do not want you to let management know."

"What do you want to change."

"I'm going to move to the third floor. That will still put me below NOA if NOA picks the fourth-floor office, and I will still be able to make my shot on Peter. I can still catch NOA coming down the stairwell. Please do not tell anyone about this I need some questions answered on this mission and I need to know I can trust you."

"I do not like this idea but I can tell you're not going to change your mind so I will go along with it, but when you explain this to management after we are done make sure to let them know I had no part in it," Chip expressed, with concern.

"I will," I said, "Thanks. It's nice to know I can trust you."

The next morning, I got up early but not to run. I wanted to pack all the bags and get them in the van, so they were ready to go. I made breakfast for me and Chip. Then we ran some more scenarios and different outcomes. I wanted to get there two hours early, but Chip would not budge on that one. Management was adamant that we followed NOA's plan. I did talk him into one hour and fifteen minutes early. This just meant I would have to work quickly but I still felt I had enough time.

Chip drove the van behind the building I would be shooting from. I threw out three bags and told him to take off. I had to hurry. First, I wanted to put a micro camera with motion detection in six of the high-profile rooms. I didn't want to rely on Chip to let me know if NOA was in the building. The motion detectors would alert my phone and I would be able to see who came into the room. I also brought the dummy shooter that we used on Jill's mission. I was going to set it up in the room I told management I was going to be in. I was on my way to my room when Chip called me. "Hey, I see you in the original room. Did you change your mind again I need to know what room to protect?"

I explained to him it was the dummy. "I told you I have to get some questions answered on this trip. I will be where I told you I would be." Then I went and set up my room for the shot. I got the room all set up. Then I told Chip I was ready to go.

I told Chip I was ready but there was still one thing left to do. I wanted to put a video recorder on the bottom level. I regretted not setting one up at the airport. I would have learned a lot more information if I would have just set up a camera to record the whole thing. So, I went down and set the camera up. Now I was ready to settle in with my gun. I was now ready to take the shot.

I thought I needed a lot of time, but we still had twenty minutes to spare before Peter and Iven were set to arrive. I spent the time checking all my cameras. Nobody was in any of the rooms. I knew it was a long shot, but I just needed to make sure. Chip came on the radio. "Here come the cars."

They came into the parking lot one after the other. There were five cars in total. Some had Iven's men. Some had Peter's men. One car for the realtors and then two limos that Iven and Peter were in. The smaller cars parked on the outside of the parking lot and the two limos parked about twenty feet apart. This left good clean shooting lanes. Peter got out of his car first and started walking toward the other car. Chip came on the radio "I think I got NOA. I see a person on the third floor of the garage."

Then management came on the radio. "Wait for NOA to take the shot. Make sure it is NOA before you shoot."

Ivan's door started to open. I started my one-minute timer. Then Iven stepped out. I put my scope on Peter's head and started tracking him toward Iven. Just then I saw a muzzle flash from the roof of the garage. That shot was too early I thought. I turned my rifle to Iven, but Iven was still alive. Then I saw another shot from the roof. It was Chip. "I think I got him" I heard him say over the radio.

Then I got the alert on my phone. My dummy had just been shot and fell over.

Peter must have seen one of the muzzle flashes too. I saw his eyes get big in my scope which was now back on him. I wanted to take the shot, but it was too late. Just then out of the window of Iven's limo came four shots. Two in the front of Peter's head, and two in the back of Iven's. I heard the limo squealing the tires as it was heading out of the parking lot.

I pulled my gun to the windshield of the limo. I was getting my first look at NOA. I could see him smiling. I almost shot just for fun, but I knew it would be a waste of a bullet. Iven and Peter's guys were already shooting up the car and I could see that the windows were bulletproof.

I got so caught up in the moment that I almost forgot that someone just tried to kill me. I left all the gear and cameras in the rooms. I grabbed the one I set up to record the whole area. I was going to want to watch that later.

I needed to get out of there fast, so I took my gun and ran one block over. I had a car waiting for me. The door was unlocked, and the keys were in the sun-visor. "See," I told myself... "Always prepare for anything."

I heard Chip on the radio asking if I was okay. I had a lot of thinking to do before I could answer Chip. I threw the radio and my cell phone out the window as I drove off.

I wanted to give it some time before I contacted Chip or management again. I knew they would be together discussing what happened and wondering where I would be. I waited until 11:00 pm that night to call Chip. I told him to walk to the bar I was going to a few nights back and to come alone.

I called him back ten minutes later. "Are you on your way?" I asked.

"I am about halfway," Chip said.

"Are you sure you are alone and not being followed?"

"Yes, I am sure."

"Good," I said, as I came up behind Chip. I started to taser him in his back as I put a chloroform rag over his mouth. "Don't fight me, Chip. This will be easier if you just let it happen."

They always show on TV that chloroform works within seconds. This is not the case. Depending on the person chloroform can take up to two or three minutes to knock a person out. That is way too long to try and hold a person of equal size. That's why I like to couple it with a stun gun. You cannot stun them for the full two or three minutes, but you can do short stuns every time they try and fight back. Chip eventually stopped trying to struggle and the chloroform did its job.

I used the key fob to open the trunk of the car that was only five feet away. Even with all Chips training, I wasn't worried about him noticing the only car on an abandoned street that never had cars. That was another reason I called his phone to keep him distracted.

It wasn't easy now that Chip was unconscious, but I managed to get him in the trunk. I threw his cell phone, wallet, watch, and his gun in a nearby trash can. I had to get rid of the gun because that morning I had put a tracking device in the bottom of his gun clip. Luckily Chip did not get in a gun fight that day because his clip was two bullets short in place of my tracker. That was the only item we always have on us so I knew it would be the best place to put it. I got rid of the rest just in case management was tracking him as well.

I drove off in the opposite direction of where I wanted to go. I wanted to drive around for a while to make sure I was not being followed. When I was comfortable, I took Chip to an abandoned house.

I had noticed multiple times on my runs this house had a garage that was detached and in the back of the house. I turned off my lights before I got to the house then I pulled back into the garage. I had to get out to manually open the garage because I did not have an opener. It was a four-car garage and was completely empty so it had plenty of room for my car and anything else I would need to do. It also had a loft on top so I could look out the window for oncoming traffic if needed.

I pulled Chip out of the trunk of the car and tied him to a chair I had placed earlier in the day. Now I just had to sit and wait for Chip to wake up. It was taking longer than I expected but I had nowhere else to be.

Finally, Chip started to come around. "What in the hell is going on! Why did you stun and drug me?" Chip yelled.

"Who did you tell, Chip?"

"Who did I tell what? Man, am I glad to see you are okay. After I saw that guy shoot and Iven and Peter were still standing, I was not sure what to think or who was shot."

"Did you get the guy that shot at me? The guy on the top of the garage?" I asked.

"No, I didn't. There was some broken glass and a tiny bit of blood, but no body. We think I hit the scope of his gun."

"Some kind of backup you are. This is why from now on I will be working alone."

"Hey, I saw the guy before the shot was fired if management wouldn't have made me wait to shoot, I would have saved you. Anyways you're not dead so what is all this about."

"Well, that leads me back to my question. Who did you tell, Chip?"

"Nobody," Chip said.

"Don't lie to me!"

"I never thought they would try and kill you or I would have shot sooner. They knew what room you would be in."

"That's it, Chip. The dummy they shot was not in the room I was supposed to be in. It was in the room I told you I would be in. I made the dummy obvious in the room we told management, but I made it hard to see in the room I told you. The only way anyone would know it was there was if they knew to look," I said, disgusted.

"I'm truly sorry. I didn't know they would try and kill you," Chip said.

"You know I can never trust you again and there is no way for me to know if you were or were not in on this."

"I know, but I was just doing my job."

"We are partners Chip if we cannot trust each other one hundred percent then we cannot be partners."

"I see that now. I thought my duty was to management not you, but now I know that is wrong."

"So do I have to kill all three of the managers? Were they all in on it?"

"I don't know. I only talked to Number Two. Number Two was the only one I told about the mission change, but I cannot tell you if the others knew or not."

"Okay, thanks," I said.

"It sucks it came down to this. I would have liked to catch that NOA bastard. Please promise me you will still get NOA someday."

I laughed. Chip was never very observant. I smiled at him and nodded my head to the right. Then I pulled the black bag that was over his head off.

"Who the hell is that?" Chip yelled.

"It's NOA. I told you I was not in either room. I stayed outside the building. I didn't care about killing Peter I wanted to catch NOA. After NOA shot Iven and Peter I was able to put a tracking device on his car. I followed him back to the same rental car place that you and the other driver used last time."

"Did you already kill him?"

"No, I shot him in the leg before I tasered and chloroformed him. That is where the blood is from. I left him in the trunk of the car the rest of the day but when I had to get you, I gave him some ketamine so, NOA will be out for a while longer."

Chip smiled and said "Thanks for this. It almost makes it worth it. Hey, I want to let you know I forgive you. Don't let this ruin your life. Don't start drinking again either. I want you to find a life outside of the job."

"Thanks, I'm not sure I can do that, but thanks."

Then I raised the gun and it happened. I always worried if I could live with myself if I killed random women and children, and now my first kill ever by my own hands was my best friend in the world and there was no way I could take it back.

The percussion from the shot must have started to wake NOA. I had to turn and wipe the tears from my eyes.

"Wait a minute," Nicole said. Who had been quietly listing to the story to this point.

"You talked about Chip. Chip is not dead."

"Chip is an acronym. You know the new crappie Chip, not the old good one," I said.

"Okay, sorry...continue," Nicole said.

Like I said, the percussion from the shot must have started to wake NOA. I had to turn and wipe the tears from my eyes. I walked behind his chair so NOA could not see me. I was surprised at how little struggle and fight NOA put up. His hands and wrist were tied to the chair. You could see the confusion in his face, but it didn't last long. It was amazing how fast NOA calmed himself and accepted his situation.

"Your dam good at your job," I said, to get the conversation started.

"Obviously not as good as you. Why am I still alive do you want to hear me beg for my life or something? Because I don't think you're going to get that."

"Why do you not fear death, or do you just feel your life is not worth begging for?"

"Neither of them. It's just when you take on this line of work you don't expect to live into your golden years. I did expect to see next week, but I guess shit happens."

"I work in your line of work, and I expect to see my golden years. I think I would at least try and see if there was a way out."

"Okay! Okay! 'Yea, though I walk through the valley of the shadow of death I shall fear no evil.' There, are you happy? I begged for my life now are you going to let me go? I didn't think so..."

"You know I find it funny that people always use that line when they think they are going to die. I don't think that verse was intended for the last moments of your life. From the time you take your first step as a baby, you are beginning your walk through the valley of the shadow of death. Every step takes you closer to it. I think that passage was meant for every day to day living. It tells you to not fear evil in your day to day. It's not just to get you out of the big oh shit situations. I think if you do that then maybe you will not get in the big oh shit situation in the first place."

"Well now is a fine time to tell me that. So, what's the verse that I use to get me out of this big oh shit situation."

"You can start by telling me who you work for and how you get your jobs," I said. My tears had dried up by now so I started to walk around to the front of his chair so I could see his face.

"Why are you messing with me? You know I get my jobs the same way you do."

"So, you don't run the job board? Aren't you the one that started the job board?"

I could see from the confused look on his face that I was not going to get an answer to any of the questions I was asking.

"Wait. You don't know who runs the job board either? We are both just competing for jobs. I was not taking away your work? So, you don't have to kill me. I will stop taking the jobs, I swear."

NOA was either a really good liar or there was no more information NOA was going to give me. I started to smile and was going to say I guess you did beg for your life after all. But I didn't. I just said, "Well even if I am not going to get information on the job board at least I get to be the one to kill NOA."

After I said that, NOA started to say, "Why are you calling me…" but I never let him finish that sentence. I put two slugs in his chest and watched him die.

I had never killed anyone in my life, and this was the second person I killed in less than an hour. It was amazing the different ranges in emotion between the two kills. The first one was the hardest thing I ever had to do even to this day, and the second was one of the most pleasurable experiences I have ever felt.

I had spent almost six months chasing NOA and I finally got him. It was a short-lived feeling. The first thing I thought after killing NOA was man, I bet Chip would have loved to see that. Then I looked over at his lifeless body sitting in the chair, and all the guilt started to pour back over me. The only way I was going to get rid of that was to get back to work.

The next step was to call management. I let them know I had captured NOA. I gave them my location and told them to come alone. They tried to ask me a bunch of questions on the phone, but I just hung up on them after I gave them the location.

It took them about thirty minutes to get to me. I watched them from up in the loft as they came in to make sure they were alone. They were alone so I yelled at them to open the garage door and let themselves in. After they were in, I told them to shut the garage door behind them. I hid a camera so I could stay in the loft and watch their reactions to finding Chip and NOA. I already knew Number Two was not leaving here alive, but I needed to try and figure out if Number One and Three also knew about my location.

It was obvious from his face that Number Two knew NOA. There was more of a disappointment in seeing Chip's body than a surprise. Number One and Three seemed truly surprised to see Chip dead. They had a more curious look about NOA. It was the opposite reaction of Number Two. They started asking questions like who's this guy and why would he kill Chip. After a few minutes, Number Two started to look very concerned and then said. "We need to get out of here. If he killed Chip, we could be next. This man is obviously not stable."

Number Two started to look around for an exit, but I had seen all I needed to see. I started to walk down the stairs and yelled out, "Where are you going?"

Number Two was getting more and more agitated.

"What's the meaning of this? Why is Chip dead and who is this guy?" Number Three asked.

"Why don't you ask Number Two?" I said.

Number Two looked around and said, "How would I know." Then did something I did not expect. Number Two reached behind his back and started to pull out a gun.

I already had mine out and pointed at him so all I had to do was pull the trigger. His gun never made it far enough around to come close to hitting me, but his finger still pulled the trigger and fired off a shot. You could see the surprise and the confusion on Number One and Three. Both for the fact that I had just shot

Number Two and that Number Two had a gun of his own.

They both looked at me in amazement and fear wondering if they were going to be next. So, I asked them the question, "Do I need to kill you two as well? Were you also in on this?"

"In on what?" Number One asked.

"So, you do not know who that is?" I asked.

They both shook their heads no.

"It is NOA," I said.

I started to explain to them the story of what happened earlier in the day and how I ended up following and capturing NOA.

"But why is Chip dead, then?" Number One asked.

I then explained to them how I moved rooms. "Chip told me his only communication was with Number Two, and that is why Number Two is dead. Now I need to know what you guys know before I can decide if you need to die as well?"

"Why would we want you dead? We spent a lot of time and effort training you just to kill you off. What sense does that make?" Number One asked.

"At this point, I am sure there is nothing we can say or do to convince you, so either shoot us or let us get on with our day," Number Three said.

"I can say if you kill all of us you will be running for the rest of your life. The company will never stop looking for you. I did see Number Two going for his gun first. You acted in self-defense, and it is still going to take a lot of convincing and some harder evidence than you have told me so far, but right now we are your only chance of a somewhat normal life." Number One said.

I had already made up my mind before I walked down the stairs that I was going to let them live but I guess I just had to make sure. I lowered my gun and said, "I guess you guys are okay."

Then I took them upstairs to watch the video of them looking at Chip and NOA for the first time. They could still not believe that Number Two would want me killed but agreed that his face did show everything I described.

"They called in the cleanup crew for Chip and NOA and the rest is history. That's how I got started in this line of work," I said, to Nicole.

"Well, it is a very interesting story. I get the feeling that the man in the story is a lot different than the man I am talking to now," Nicole said.

There was nothing I could say to reply to that, but it was a very true statement.

Chapter Nine
Still Back Home

Nicole was behind on preparing dinner. She had just spent most of the afternoon talking on the phone listening to a story. Niles would be home any minute. They ate dinner and cleaned up the dishes. Niles played with the kids until bedtime then, Nicole put them to bed.

While they were lying in bed, Nicole turned to Niles and said, "Are you getting tired of the same old thing every day? Why don't you quit your job tomorrow and not go on your business trip? We will just pack up and move to Europe tomorrow."

This agitated Niles. Nicole knew it would, but she had to try.

"Where is this coming from you have never said you're not happy before? How would we afford the move, and how would I find a job in Europe?"

Nicole could see how agitated Niles was becoming so she just let it go.

"It's okay honey it was just a thought. I am not unhappy. We have just been doing the same thing for some time now and change might be nice, but I know you don't like change so we can come back to this after your trip. Sleep well."

Nicole said to sleep well, but Niles did not sleep well that night. Her words just kept replaying all night in his head. The next morning Niles tried to act like nothing was wrong, but it was not fooling Nicole. She was not in the mood to put up with him being a baby. So, she just went along with the charade and let Niles leave for his business trip like nothing was wrong.

Chapter Ten
The Last Mission

He had just gotten off the phone with Chip after he killed Ariane and her father Nicolas. Chip told him to get to the meeting place. The meeting place was across town at another small hotel. He walked into the room with the room key he already had. He expected to see Chip but was completely confused when he saw Nicole sitting in a chair across the room.

"What the hell are you doing here?" he asked.

"Why did you kill her?" Nicole said.

"What do you mean why did I kill who? You shouldn't be here. How did you get here? None of this makes sense."

"Why did you kill Ariane?"

"How do you know about Ariane? What the hell is going on?" he asked.

"Tell me why you killed her. You had no reason to kill her. She was not part of the mission. I will explain everything to you but first I need to know why you killed Ariane?"

He was now walking around the room franticly. He was very uncomfortable and very confused. His gut feeling was to just go to the door and leave but he had too many questions. His mind was racing, and his emotions were all over the place. Then Nicole said, "For the last time I need an answer if you do not answer me, I am going to leave and let you deal with the company on your own?"

"How can you help me with the company I just told you about them last week?" he asked.

Nicole got up out of her chair and started walking toward the door. "If you're not going to answer me then I have to leave." She grabbed the handle and started to open it when he said, "I killed her because she is not you."

Nicole shut the door and walked back over to him and said, "What do you mean, you killed her because she was not me?"

"I do not know. Ever since we talked last week, I have not been able to stop thinking about you. When I was with her, I felt like I was cheating on you, but I also found myself enjoying her company. I kept thinking why can't I be with someone like this? You are married I can't be with you."

He kept his head facing down to the ground the whole time he was walking back and forth. He would not look at Nicole at all.

"I think in the end I just know I want to be with you so if Ariane is no longer around then I no longer have a choice to make. I can't let anyone disrespect you. She should not have made me cheat on you," he said.

He started getting more agitated as he talked. He was now slapping himself in the face.

"I know none of this makes any sense. I just met you a week ago, but I feel like I have known you forever."

Nicole stood up and walked over to him. She put her hand on his face and looked him in the eye and said, "It's all right. One last thing I need to know. Last week when you told me the story about NOA you said you put a tracker on his car and that is how you followed him back to the rental car return place. That is not true, is it? You wouldn't have had time to put a tracker on his car. So how did you know where to find him?"

"You are starting to creep me out," he said, as he took a few steps back from her. A smile came across his face and he said, "What the hell. I have never told anyone this. I did not want the company to know so I always told the story with me putting a tracker on the car. I never put a tracker on the car."

"Then how did you know where to find him at," Nicole questioned.

"My long runs," he said, with a smile. "I have always been paranoid of the company. I always felt like they were watching my every move. I found it odd that they did not want me to investigate the rental car company from the airport. I knew if I just drove there and started asking questions, they would know I disobeyed Number Two's order and did not leave it alone. I had to make sure I could go there and do my investigation without anyone knowing. It's hard to tell if someone is following you in a car but not when you are running. It is easy to know if you are being watched. The first week I would just go on random short runs to see if I was followed. I was the first few times, but after a week and a half of random running, they must have thought it was not worth their time and they just let me run. Once they stopped following me, all I had to do was run to the rental car place and do my investigation. The kid at the counter was new. The first thing I did was ask to rent the black limo that was in the back lot. When the kid told me, they were reserved for a private company, and I could not rent them. It was easy to put two and two together. All I had to do then was give the kid a couple hundred dollars and my burner cell phone number. I told him if I got a call the next time the limos went out there would be another two hundred thrown his way. I knew that morning when the limo left the lot that NOA would be returning it there, but I still needed to see how everything was going to play out at the site. I also gave the kid a few hundred more dollars to leave me a rental car with the keys in the visor at a location just down the street from where we were going to shoot Iven and Peter.

Nicole smiled and said, "We always wondered how you found him."

"What do you mean? Tell me what is going on," he said, with panic in his voice.

"What is your name?" Nicole asked.

"You know my name. Why are you asking me that?"

"Really, you think you have told me your name. You have not. Tell me what it is now."

"My name is. Um… It's," he pondered.

"You can't tell me. Can you?"

"No, I can't."

"It's because you don't have a name. Your name is "HE", Humanless Engagement. It's your acronym. This makes it easier to take on a new name for every mission you go on. If you do not have a name, you will never slip up and give the wrong one."

"But I give out my name all the time, and Chip calls me? Why can't I think what Chip calls me?" he asked.

"Chip calls you, 'He.' Just never directly to you. All the agents that work with you are trained to use generic names to address you personally. I bet you can't think of one time anyone has ever called you by name. It will always be 'hey can you come over'. But if you think about how they talk to each other I bet you will start to recall it is always 'He. He is over there. What will He be doing in this mission?'"

"Why are you telling me this? What is your part in all this?"

"You know who I am Niles. I am your wife, NICOLE. It stands for "Non-Interactive Control Off Leave Engagement", and that's the reason you feel like you love me. The only real name you have is your off-mission name "NILES." It stands for "Non-Interactive Level Engagement Specialist.""

"I am not your husband. Niles is. I met him the day I got shot at in front of the office. I talked to the bagel lady she knows Niles."

"You did not meet him you saw your reflection in the glass. Niles is not capable of handling that situation. Niles ducked down with fear and could not move. You had to come out or else you both would have died. Think about the event again, did you look at Niles or did you see Niles in the glass?"

"I don't know you are confusing me," he said.

"Tell me what you do when you leave the office every day. It is the same thing every day right. You go to the pub by your apartment then you eat and go home. You think you drink too much and that's why all your nights are hard to remember, but you wake up feeling fine every morning. The real reason you don't remember your night's or even ever leaving the office is because you never leave the office. Niles does. You go in the backroom and put on your fake wig and beard. That starts the transformation to Niles. Niles comes home to me. Niles just remembers sitting in an office all day but would never be able to give any details from the day because in the daytime Niles becomes, He or you. It's a convincing beard and wig. Only a wife would know it is not real. The beard and wig on your face are what you saw in the window that day. You had not made it to the office to take it off yet. After a few gun shots, you ripped the beard and wig off your face, and He took over."

"I remember last night and the night before," he said.

"That is because you are on a mission. You never put the beard on when you are on a mission. You also will not drink on a mission it's your rule. That is why you think you remember your mission nights, and why Niles will never be able to give any real details from his work trips. Here is the beard do you want to put it on?"

"Hell no! Get that thing away from me!"

"You told me all about your first mission but that is just the parts you remember. If I had to bet, you do not have one memory from before that first night management found you in the bar. That is because that night was staged to be your first memory." "Niles", she stopped. "Oh my gosh, I don't even know your real name. Anyways," she said, as she shook her head. "Niles was found in a state asylum. You were afraid of everything. You hated your life and would not come out of the room for anything. You were also too afraid to kill yourself. You wanted to die but were so scared of death you could not function as a normal person. From what I understand one day you had enough and you snapped. You walked out of the room and tried to leave the property. Normally you were so weak that one orderly could handle you, but on this day, you disabled five orderlies and made it out of the asylum. They found you the next day curled up in an alley too scared to talk to anyone. You could not remember how you got there and just kept asking to go back to your room. Number One was onsite that day as they brought you back in. After hearing about your strength and how you took out the orderlies. Number One came up with a plan to try and make you an agent."

"How would a guy that sat in a room all day doing nothing be strong."

"It turns out that you were so scared that you kept your muscles tense at all time. While you were shivering and shaking your muscles were constantly tearing and rebuilding themselves. The weird thing was it was all your muscles, not just your upper or lower body it was even muscles that bodybuilders have trouble working out. You made yourself solid to the core. The problem was there would be no way to put you on a mission or even train you. The company started bringing in their doctors to talk to you. They tried focusing on that day you escaped but no matter what they did, not even hypnotizing you would make you remember any part of that day. Finally, they gave up on that and came up with a plan that would make you not scared of anything. I don't know how they convinced you to sign the waiver, but they got you to permit them to torture you day and night. I think they convinced you it could not be any worse than the day-to-day life you were living. The theory was they would tortured you with your worse fears day after day until you got so used to being tortured that you did not fear anything anymore. I was not there but I know they did some pretty bad things to you. Things like drowning you, beating you, hot and cold temperature changes. I believe they even shot you so you would no longer fear being shot. The first few days I think they took it easy on you with just some hot water and spiders. On the third day, they brought in some big guys to rough you up, and after a bad enough beating that is when He came out in front of them for the first time. He fought back and took them all out. I think you even killed one of them with your bare hands. I heard you did this with no remorse at all. The doctors said "He" had no fear and would take a punch without feeling any pain. The next day you did not remember anything. They continued torturing you day in and out until there was no more, *whatever your real name is*, but only He. The night you remember management meeting you at the bar happened 26 times before you retained it in your memory. The first 25 you would always wake up not remembering the day before. Even after they started training you for the NOA mission there would still be some days you would not remember, and they would have to repeat. Once you got focused and fully committed to catching NOA you never forgot a single moment from then on."

"That was the problem though. When you were off mission and had nothing to focus on you would downward spiral. You would not sleep and start to show signs of slipping back to your old personality. NOA was not a rival assassin. NOA was a secondary project training at the same time. You were both given similar missions to see how you would react and how you would plan the mission. You excelled in every way but not being able to handle yourself between missions is why Number Two wanted to have you killed. You put an end to that once you captured and killed your NOA," Nicole said.

"So that is what NOA was trying to say when I killed him. NOA thought I was NOA," he questioned.

"Yep, the other part you don't know is that NOA's old Chip is now your new Chip. Luckily your Chip only hit his scope after New Chip shot at you. That is how your new Chip got the scar on his face that you make fun of all the time. You know the one you have never asked about."

"I always knew Chip was a screw-up. Well, that will make it way easier to do what I must do now. This time will be much easier than the last."

"You have never forgiven yourself for killing Chip, have you?"

"No, I don't think so. There was no reason for him to die, but I can't change that now."

"No, I guess not, but you can learn to live with it."

"So how do you fit in all this then?" he asked.

"Well after you killed the only other assassin the company was training. They had to find a way to make you work. They knew that you could not be you off missions and the other you could not go on missions. So, they decided to deprogram you. They put you back in the same room you lived in fear in. Then they let you sit there for months until the old you started to come back. This time they gave you no contact with the outside world. They didn't even let you shave or cut your hair. Once the old you came back, they started putting lots of mirrors in the room with you so you would become accustomed to seeing yourself with a beard and long hair. They started calling you Niles and slowly making you feel comfortable again. They did the same training they did with "He", but in reverse. I think we went on ten first dates before you started to remember them. The first few "He" would come out and ruin the date. We would have to end them early. After a while, I would notice you rubbing your face when you were with me. If you felt the beard, you would calm down. Eventually, you fell in love with me, and "He" would never come out when I was around.

Then they shaved the beard and cut your hair and started torturing you again to bring "He" back out. They would only let "He" do small missions. Then they would put a fake beard and wig on you and bring me back in the picture once it was done. You eventually loved me so much that the transition became easy for you. They would never let me see you without the wig. I think this is the first time I have seen your face in years."

"What are you going to do now?" Nicole asked.

"Finish the mission. It's what I do best," he said.

"Your mission is over. Nicolas is dead."

"From what you have just told me, it looks like I just got a new Number One, and Three and Chip."

"Then what? What is after that?"

"I don't know what you want from me," he yelled.

"I want a father for my children, but I can no longer put up with that wimp. I need a man that is strong and confident but not hateful. I want you to make love to me like you made love to that girl you just killed, but I also need someone that is there for me and not always thinking about himself. I want the best of Niles and He not the worst of both. Our children deserve that too," Nicole said.

"This is a lot. I don't know if I can do that right now. Just let me go finish what I must do then I will try and learn how to live that way."

"That's the problem. It's always about both of you. Well, you don't have the luxury of that today. I have our kids safe right now, but I have been sent to kill you. This experiment is over from the company's eyes. I am sorry. I did not mean to have children with you. I was told that I couldn't have children. That is one of the reasons I was chosen for this mission. Our kids are a miracle, and I cannot help loving you for giving them to me. I want us both to leave and run away together. I have things in motion. We can live together forever but for that, to work you must convince me in the next five minutes that you can be the best of both. Because while I do love you, I still love my kids more. I need your help to keep them safe from the company, but I do not need to keep them safe from the company if you are not around."

"You would kill me?" he asked.

"Please don't make me," Nicole said with tears running down her face.

"I won't," he said, as He kissed her on her forehead.

"But I also don't think I can be both," he said, as He picked up his gun and put it to his head.

"I truly do think we both love you, but this is best for all. I know what it is like killing someone you love, and I would never put you through that," he said, as he moved over to the door. He opened the door and slammed it shut....

The End

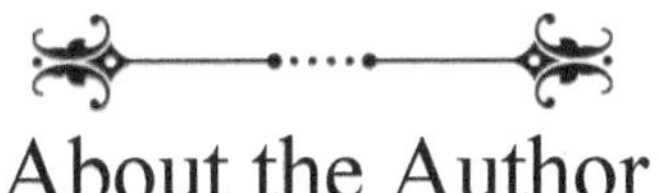

About the Author

Born and raised a Colorado native Vern Kaska III is a networking professional whose job has taken him all over the world implementing network designs for his customers. His first loves are God and his family, his wife Jen of over 20 years, and his son Lance. His second love is the outdoors where most of his free time is spent.